Sherlock Holmes:
For Letter or Verse

Joseph W. Svec III

Paperback ISBN 978-1-80424-595-8
ePub ISBN 978-1-80424-596-5
PDF ISBN 978-1-80424-597-2

Published by MX Publishing
335 Princess Park Manor, Royal Drive,
London, N11 3GX
www.mxpublishing.co.uk

Cover design by Awan

Dedication

This book is dedicated to my beautiful wife, best friend, and soulmate Lidia. Thank you for your love and inspiration.

Table of Contents

Introduction

Welcome Sherlockian enthusiasts to a fascinating collection of letter-based Sherlock Holmes mysteries, interspersed with a unique gathering of rhymed and metered Sherlock Holmes poems. These letter-based mysteries were originally presented in the "Dear Holmes" subscription-based mysteries by mail service, which provides readers with a new Victorian era mystery to solve each month, through letters sent by Sherlock's clients or others. The first letter presents the mystery along with various clues, and possible suspects. Each additional letter provides more clues and information, giving the reader the opportunity to solve the mystery before they receive their final letter from Sherlock Holmes, in which he provides the solution, and how he came to that conclusion. Readers are invited to send their solutions to "Dear Holmes" to see how they fared against other detective subscribers and Sherlock Holmes himself, and each month a featured detective is chosen, based on how accurate their solution was. So, as you read the letter-based mysteries, put on your deerstalker hat, and enjoy seeing the mystery unfold with each new letter until it is solved. Then it is time to take a break with a rhymed and metered Sherlock Holmes story poem, before you begin your next letter-based mystery.

Sherlock Holmes: "For Letter or Verse"

"Welcome", said the gracious host.
"Come in and sit a spell.
We will go through Sherlock's post,
their stories for to tell.

It's not well known, but you will see,
that many cases strange,
were solved in daily post", said he.
"How's that for a change?"

"A Dr. Watson's thrilling tale
Intrigue's us. Yes, it's true,
but in Sherlocks daily mail,
now, there is something new.

Without any added flair,
or Watson's "extra" touch,
the letters by themselves do share,
oh, so very much.

From start, to finish, when it's solved,
mystery, it beckons.
In his post, It's quite evolved.
The answer clearly reckons.

So sit back, and listen now,
to tales I will recite,
of shades, and phantoms, and somehow,
of robberies in the night.

But please, my reader, do not fear,
I will not be terse.
Let me make it truly clear,
I will add some verse.

Some Sherlock tales in metered rhyme,
to lighten up the day.
This is also what I am
going to share this day.

For letter or verse you'll get both,
I will be forthright.
I have made my solemn oath,
So read on, in delight!

Sherlock Holmes and
The Case of the Missing Rhyme

I sat trembling with pen in hand,
at my paper, staring oer' the land,
wondering what word to use,
to complete the rhyme that I did choose.

Yet I could not find it.
I could not never mind it.
Who could help me in this chore?
Is it like a Sign of Four?

Or a Scarlet Thread upon the chair?
Where to look I knew not where.
Would it be in the Valley of Fear?
Is there a vicious hound? Oh Dear!

T'would be a Scandal, Bohemian, I am sure
if the rhyme I could not procure.
I'd blush like a league of red heads you see,
or even loose my identity.

Could it be in Boscome Valley somewhere,
beneath Five Orange Pips over there?
I really must get a grip.
Should I ask the Man with the Twisted Lip?

Or perhaps the goose that ate the Carbuncle Blue
would know exactly just what I should do.
I had the rhyme almost at hand,
but it slipped away like a Speckled Band.

Perhaps if I have just a we bit o' rum
I can nail it like an Engineer's Thumb.
Or if I search the world global
I will find it like a Bachelor Noble

If I were trying to rhyme with Beryl Cornet
Ha! It t'would really be no sweat.
As easy as rhyming with Copper Beeches
Just a bowl of tasty peaches.

But here I stand with out my rhyme.
What to do, truly lost I am.
About it make no bones at all,
Sherlock Holmes is the one to call.

Sherlock Holmes and
the New Haven Night Stalker

1st letter:

William Worthington, Tea Merchant
53 Wellington Rd.
Newhaven, England

Dear Mr. Holmes,

I hope this letter finds you well. While you do not know me, you are a legend in the world of tea merchants. Being that some things are better left unsaid, I can only allude to your resolution of a certain situation that involved the possibility of a vampire.

While all the obvious facts seemed to leave no doubt, you quickly dispelled the possibility of such a horrible conclusion. It is this same terrifying subject, upon which I find myself writing to you on. There is no other way to say this, but I believe my new daughter-in-law is a vampire.

My 18-year-old son, Jamie has always been very close to me. We have shared many a special times together over the years. However, three years ago, when our second child was born, Jamie grew somewhat cold and distant. He seemed to bear a resentment and hostility towards his younger brother. He finally expressed a desire to go away for a while, and see the world, so using my connections in the shipping industry, I was able to secure for him a position as a cabin boy in one of the very best ships in the tea trade. The ship's master was an old friend of mine.

Jamie took to the sea and his shipboard duties quite well, and in all the reports I received, the captain spoke very highly of him. When his term was finished, he signed up for a second voyage, much to my surprise, and everything seemed to be going rather positively. You can imagine my even greater surprise when he showed up at my doorstep recently and introduced to me his new wife.

He had met her while ashore on one of his voyages and was instantly smitten with her. They were married while he was on leave, and she somehow convinced the captain to let her join Jamie on board for the remainder of the trip. That was quite unexpected because the captain is a very traditional man and set in his ways. I would have never imagined that he would allow a woman aboard his ship.

I must say, her appearance is somewhat strange. In spite of her extremely pale skin, and her long white hair, she is rather attractive in an unusual way, and I can understand why Jamie may have been drawn to her. She has an almost hypnotic look about her. I have been told that she is from the Baltic area of Europe, somewhere near Wallachia, Romania, and is in some way related to a well-known count or other upper-class family that has fallen on hard times. They were not clear about that particular point, but her guardian seemed most pleased with her marriage to Jamie. She is very quiet and withdrawn and seems to sleep a great deal. My son says it is merely her unfamiliarity with our climate, customs, and country, but I sense that something is just not right with her.

Since his return, on more than one occasion I have woken up in the middle of the night, and glanced out my bedroom window, to see someone that looked a great deal like his wife, walking about the grounds outside. I looked again, and the mysterious figure had disappeared. One night, I even went downstairs and searched the grounds, but I saw no one. When I questioned my son, he insisted that she was in bed with him the entire night. They went to sleep together, and she was always there when he woke up, so he is certain she never left the room. I cannot imagine why he would lie to me about the subject, but he is quite adamant about it.

One other point of interest is that Jamie no longer bears any animosity, or jealousy towards his younger brother. Jamie's behavior towards him has been irreproachable. He is most kind and regales him with stories of his travels to far-off lands, and his sea voyages. He even gave him a child-size sailor's outfit, as well as some lovely antique toys that he had brought back from his travels. Little William is very much enthralled with his new gifts and is always playing with them.

At least he was until he took ill. William had been in excellent health and enjoyed climbing the trees that were recently planted on our grounds. However just after Jamie's return, he fell sick and has started growing weaker and weaker. He also has repeated nightmares about a lady in white hovering over him. When we go to him, he is all alone, but I cannot help but wonder if my son's new wife is somehow causing the illness. I hesitate to say this, but I believe that she may be a vampire, and she is draining the life from my son. I know this sounds improbable, if not impossible, however, it is more than coincidental that he should fall ill, and have these nightmares of a lady in white, right after my son returns home with his unusual new bride. And she fits the description of the woman in little William's nightmares. What am I to do?

Your deduction skills are legendary, Mr Holmes. I must call upon you to help me in this terrifying conundrum that is life-threatening to my son. The local doctor has no answer as to what might be causing the illness, and William just keeps getting sicker every day. The only thing that is keeping him happy is the new toys that he has with him constantly. I would be eternally indebted to you if you could in some way help me resolve this situation.

Yours,
William Worthington

2nd letter:

Dr. John Watson, MD
From the home of William Worthington
53 Wellington Rd.
Newhaven, England

Dear Holmes,

Per your request, I have taken the train down to Newhaven, to investigate the rather questionable claims of William Worthington. If you had not been so busy with the other unusual cases that happened to be demanding your time presently, I am sure you would have had this resolved by now. I really do not understand why claims of a demon dog or werewolf or some other such nonsense would take precedence over saving the life of a sick child whose delusional father attributes it to an impossible legendary creature. No one takes vampires seriously. If this keeps up, you may have to revise your rule, "No ghosts need apply" to "No one who believes in ghosts, werewolves, vampires, or other ridiculous figments of the imagination, need apply." Really Holmes, I could have been enjoying a nice quiet evening at home instead of chasing about Newhaven seeking answers to this nonsense. Whatever it is that is causing the illness, I am certain it is not a vampire.

But since I am here, I did look into each of the particular items you asked me to. As you had cautioned me, I was very careful not to raise suspicions in my investigations. I do not think anyone suspects what you had initially determined.

I examined the young boy quite thoroughly, and decided that, exactly as you thought, somehow, he has been exposed to a deadly toxic substance. My treatment is helping him, but he is not out of the woods yet. I have not yet determined the origin or nature of the poison, but I am still working on it. Knowing what it is will make it much easier to treat, and I am certain aid in speeding his full recovery.

Along with this letter, you will find three small envelopes. The first contains scrapings of the paint from the toys his brother gave to him. As you had mentioned, if the older brother still harbors ill intentions toward the youngster, providing toys with a poisonous substance on them would be a perfect way to secretly administer the toxin. As soon as you determine if that is the cause, do let me know what the toxin is, so I can adjust his treatment.

I also removed some threads from the child's sailor outfit his brother gave him. They are in the second envelope. As you surmised that too could be a way to administer the poison topically. The child had been wearing the outfit quite regularly while his brother regaled him with stories of his adventures across the seven seas.

Regarding Jamie's rather unusual new bride, although quite fetching in an odd way, she certainly is a strange one. She speaks very little, but when she does, her voice is almost hypnotic. I can see how she convinced Mr. Worthington's captain friend to let her aboard the ship. And she has the most piercing eyes. They are like a spider's web. They draw you in until you really don't know what you are doing or saying. I have honestly had to be overly cautious in her presence. While I am not at all implying, she is the cause of all this, if there were such a thing as a vampire, I say she would fit the image perfectly. I have not yet caught her anywhere near young William. Since I arrived, I have spent the nights watching over him. It is to monitor his condition, of course, but also to see if she is surreptitiously visiting him during the night. So far, she has not been in his room.

The mother is more than beside herself with concern and has been suffering from exhaustion and anxiety about her child's health. She was positively frantic by the time I arrived, so I prescribed a sedative, and assured her that I would watch over things. She is finally sleeping better.

Mr. Worthington has been extremely quiet. I would say to a concerning level. I have tried to dissuade him from persisting in his belief that his daughter-in-law is a vampire, but he watches his son's bride constantly, and I am certain he still believes that she is the cause of all this. I just hope he does not do anything rash before you can decide if what you suspect, is indeed the case.

The final envelope, as you requested, contains some samples of the bark, leaves and berries from the new trees that were planted on the Worthington's property. These are the trees the young boy had been playing and climbing on prior to falling ill. Yes, I was quite careful and wore gloves while collecting the samples. I also made some inquiries about the source of the trees. That is the most interesting part. They were a gift from an anonymous source. They arrived one day by a portage service, and the labor to plant them was also a part of the delivery. A team of laborers accompanied the freight wagon and planted the trees where Mr. Worthington instructed them. They even planted some lovely purple flowers around them and then left with the delivery wagon. I have included the packing slip and the note that came with the trees. As you can see, all it says, is "Enjoy the trees. You certainly deserve them!" Mr. Worthington has made inquiries with several of his clients, but so far, no one admits to sending the trees. I am certain that you only need to refer to your recent monograph on handwriting analysis to determine who wrote it, when it was written, whether the author was right or left-handed, and what he had for dinner.

I believe that is everything that you requested. I shall remain here to watch over the child and make sure Mr. Worthington does not do anything he will later regret. If you can drag yourself away from dog-catching duty on that werewolf case, I would appreciate your expeditious response. I anxiously await your reply. My warm and comfortable bed awaits me.

Yours,
John Watson

3rd letter:

William Worthington, Tea Merchant
53 Wellington Rd.
Newhaven, England

Dear Mr. Holmes,

I was relieved beyond measure to receive your letter, delivered by your associate Dr. Watson, about my son's condition. Under the good doctor's care, William has stabilized somewhat, and is not getting any worse, but he is still very weak. The doctor has been staying at his bedside with him every night, which precludes any nocturnal visits by anyone else. (If you know what I mean.)

It was reassuring to know, that in your preliminary analysis, you have ruled out vampires. I do understand how unlikely the possibility of my son's wife being a vampire is. However, considering that just after she arrived, poor, little William came down with this inexplicable illness, and her more than unusual appearance, it seemed like almost a certainty. I am still not fully convinced otherwise and have been keeping my eye on her when possible, making sure that she is never alone with my young son.

Dr. Watson did mention that you while you are involved in another important case that prevents you from being here in person, you are still working on resolving the danger to my son. I am not certain how that is possible all the way from London, but you are the expert. Still, I look forward to your presence, and I am certain you will bring this to a successful resolution.

I cannot imagine why, but Dr. Watson had asked me to

contact the portage service that delivered the trees that were recently planted on our property, to investigate the source of them, and perhaps discover any pertinent information. I believe he has communicated to you that they were an anonymous delivery, and we still have not determined from whom they were sent. The trees and the workers to plant them showed up at the office of the freighting service, with payment and instructions to deliver them here to me. I was pleasantly surprised when they arrived, but did not suspect anything amiss at the time. After all, how can some simple, young trees cause any harm? And the lovely purple flowers that were planted with them are quite beautiful.

I have also tried to locate the laborers who planted them. I thought, perhaps, if I spoke to them, they could reveal some bit of information that might be helpful. The odd thing is that the two men who accompanied the wagon and handled the planting, seem to have vanished. They were not local fellows. That, I can say for certain, as I am acquainted with most of the residents of the area, and they had a rather heavy foreign accent. It sounded remarkably similar to the accent of my son's wife, but it is hard to confirm, as she really does not speak very often.

I have also been able to learn a bit more about her. It turns out; she is a descendant of a Romanian count. Due to some unspeakable, tragic event in the past, her family lost all of their wealth. She had lived with her guardian, a Mr. Florescu, prior to marrying my son. She brought nothing of material or financial value to the marriage, but as we are quite well-off with my tea importing business, it really does not matter. In fact, when I have passed on, the business and all our property will be divided between my two sons, and they will be well taken care of.

Jamie does seem incredibly happy, and quite in love with her despite my reservations. I did discover that the reason she often sleeps during the daytime, is that she is taking medication for some medical condition. He did not tell me what is wrong with her, but I did find out that her medication is paraldehyde. I am not familiar with it. Perhaps you would know if this has any bearing on the situation.

In my conversations with Dr. Watson, he has mentioned that your insight and analysis of even the smallest details have often been the critical deciding factor in your investigations. Many times, you have observed some minute, seemingly insignificant piece of information, which turns out to be the most important. It is with that in mind that I mention one additional item.

Just before Jamie returned, and William fell ill, I had received a rather odd business proposition. It offered to make a most substantial tea purchase, but the buyer wanted to meet me and my wife in person prior to completing the sale. The letter stated that while was it just a formality, the buyer was most insistent that we both attend the meeting. On Tuesday next week, my wife and I are to meet the buyer's representative at the docks in Newhaven Harbour, in East Sussex, and find the Romanian steam yacht, The Balaur, where the meeting will be held on board. Once the meeting and formalities are concluded, the purchase is to be completed.

I would normally hesitate to make such a trip, and to inconvenience my wife, especially with little William being so sick, but the purchase they offered is quite substantial. In all my years as a tea merchant, I have never received such an odd sales offer. I would not have even mentioned it, were it not for the meeting location being on board a Romanian yacht, and my son's new wife being from the same country. It seems to be too much of a coincidence. Would you not agree? Should I move forward with this sales transaction? I have enclosed the business proposal letter for your examination. I thank you for your time and efforts and look forward to hearing from you soon.

Sincerely yours,
William Worthington

3rd Letter addendum:

Mortnum & Fason Tea Company
V. Ucserolf
Purchasing Manager

Dear Mr. Worthington,

I write you regarding tea purchase that our company want to make. You are tea broker highly recommended.

We want to purchase 5000 hundredweight of tea as soon as possible.

However, before we complete purchase, our company president want to meet you and your wife in person. This just formality, but it is tradition and must be done prior to close deal.

The meeting will take place at 5:00 pm, on Romanian yacht, The Balaur, this Tuesday at the docks in Newhaven Harbour. It is most imperative you and your wife attend. I meet you there.

V. Ucserolf

4th letter:

Dr. John Watson, MD
From the home of William Worthington
53 Wellington Rd.
Newhaven, England

Dear Holmes,

I have received your letter, and I am glad to hear that you resolved the supposed "werewolf" case you have been working on, and that it was in fact, nothing of the sort. Now that your dog-catching task is completed, we can bring this equally improbable adventure to a close.

I see that your analysis of the paint from the toys, and the threads from the child's sailor outfit is negative for toxic substances. I would agree that it is looking less likely that the older brother is the culprit. He has not shown any animosity, at least that I have observed towards his younger brother.

With the toys and sailor's outfit excluded, I was quite surprised that the examination of the samples from the mysterious trees that were delivered, also turned out to be negative. Their odd origin, and the young boy's contact with them prior to falling ill, certainly made them suspect.

I will say, I was rather shocked to discover that you paid a nocturnal visit to Mr. Worthington's gardens, without even stopping in to let me know you were here. I do understand that time was of the essence, and you had to gather your samples and get them back to Baker Street, to analyze them as soon as possible. That was very observant of you to deduce that the only remaining possible source of the boy's illness, was the purple flowers that were planted at the same time as the trees. They were so inconsequential, if quite lovely, that no one, but you, thought to even consider them. Who would have guessed that they are Monkshood, or Wolfsbane, as they are locally known, and that was the cause? You will be pleased to hear, that now that I know what the toxin is, and have modified his treatment accordingly, the boy's health is improving considerably.

However, per your rather cryptic instructions, he is being kept isolated in his room, and no one outside the immediate family is aware that he is recovering. Also, as you directed, Mr. Worthington has responded affirmatively to the mysterious business meeting proposal, and he and his wife are scheduled to meet the buyer's representative at the docks in Newhaven Harbour, on Tuesday. Mr. Worthington has provided me one of his suits, which fits me reasonably well, and I have obtained an outfit from Mrs. Worthington, for your costume. She did give me quite the odd look when I requested it. Based on your previous masquerades, I am sure you will be able to play her part quite admirably.

I have to say, that it is a rather clever ruse to disguise ourselves as Mr. and Mrs. Worthington to find out who is behind the invitation and determine if the mysterious buyer is also the one behind the poisonous flowers. That was very observant of you to notice that the name of the purchasing manager just happens to be the name of Jamies's wife's guardian spelled backwards. Is it possible, that she is involved also? If it is as you suspect, you do know, we will be walking right into a trap. And considering they attempted to poison a mere child; we are well aware that they would not hesitate to try to murder us.

You will be pleased to know, I do have my service revolver

with me, and I will bring it along. I have made arrangements to have a room available at a nearby seaside inn, so you can don your Mrs. Worthington attire before the meeting. Do you think we should contact the local authorities, and ask them to be on hand, just in case things get ugly?

Mr. Worthington has briefed me on the overall workings of his tea importing business, and the general nature of a tea purchase transaction, so I should be able to play his role without suspicion. I am sure you will have no problem playing Mrs. Worthington. The London theater suffered a great loss when you chose to be a detective.

That is all for now. I look forward to meeting you at the Newhaven docks at the time, and location that you specified.

Yours,
John Watson

5th Letter:

Sherlock Holmes
Consulting Detective
221-b Baker Street,
London, England

Dear Mr. Worthington,

You may put your mind at ease in all matters that you contacted me about in your recent letter. I am pleased to inform you; everything has been successfully resolved.

William's illness and the mysterious tea purchase letter were indeed connected. Both were perpetrated by the same party, your son's wife's former guardian. I assure you, your son's new bride is not a vampire, and was not at all responsible for any of the nefarious goings on. While her appearance may be somewhat unusual, in some ways, she was also a victim of this villainous scheme, and her life was in danger as well. In fact, all your lives were in very grave danger.

My analysis of the handwriting on the rather poorly written tea purchase letter, and the note that accompanied the trees proved they were both written by the very same person, her shadowy guardian, a Mr. Vlad Florescu. Using my wide ranging and considerable network, I was able to obtain a document he had previously written and compare it with the writing from the purchase letter and tree note. They were a perfect match.

Taking advantage of her unusual, yet captivating appearance, he came up with the idea of marrying her to an unsuspecting, well-to-do young man, and then eliminating her husband, so she would inherit his estate. Then, if she were to die suddenly, as her only living relative, the entire fortune would be his. Of course, there could be no other heirs to you and your wife, so he came up with the plan of using the poisonous flowers to kill Jamie's younger brother. By focusing the delivery on the trees, he was easily able to plant the flowers with no one giving them a second thought. Wolfsbane is a very deadly plant, especially for a young child. Had my associate Dr. Watson, not treated him, your younger son would not have survived.

The plan was to eliminate William, the second heir to your estate, and then lure you and your wife to a meeting on board the buyer's steam yacht, The Balaur. Incidentally, the Romanian word Balaur, translates to "dragon." An unfortunate explosion on board the vessel was planned to eliminate you and your wife, leaving Jamie and his new bride to inherit everything. I assure you, they would not have lived very long, had we not foiled his plan.

While his scheme was reasonably well conceived, he was ineffectual in his execution of the purchase letter. His poor English grammar can be excused, but simply spelling his name backwards did nothing to hide his identity. And the name of the supposed tea company was worse than inept. Taking the name of one of England's most famous tea companies, Fortnum & Mason, and just switching the first letters of the two words screamed incompetence.

Mr. Florescu and his Romanian accomplice were not expecting myself and Dr. Watson, in the place of a distraught tea merchant, and his defenseless wife. The good Doctor and I were easily able to overwhelm the villains when they attempted to spring their trap. Once they were subdued, we conveyed them to the authorities. From your first letter, I had deduced his plan, and when I related it to him, he confessed to everything. They are now behind bars, and no longer a threat to your family.

There is one more item of interest that I should explain. You mentioned seeing someone, that you suspected to be your son's wife, wandering about the grounds in the middle of the night, and William having nightmares of a lady in white hovering over him. This can be explained by her medical condition, somnambulism, more commonly known as sleepwalking. People who are afflicted can walk considerable distances while sleeping, with no recollection of where they have been, or what they may have done. She undoubtedly wandered into Jamie's room, as well as out onto the grounds of your property, and would never have known a thing. She then returned to her bed and woke up in the morning none the wiser. You mentioned that she is taking paraldehyde, which was my clue. It is quite often used to treat that condition. I would suggest that her door be locked at night, for her own safety.

As I have always said, one does not need to seek supernatural explanations, for what can easily be explained by clear and rational observation. I wish you well.

Yours,
Sherlock Holmes
Consulting Detective

Sherlock Holmes and
the Return of the Missing Rhyme

Once more I sat with pen in hand
Staring out across the land.
The rhyme was gone, completely lost.
It must be found at any cost!

To complete the poem, unfinished still,
It seemed a never-endless hill.
The night was quiet as a mouse,
somewhat like an Empty House.

I could turn to the Norwood Builder,
even though it would bewilder.
More than a troop of Dancing Men,
If not now, who knows when.

Perhaps a Solitary Cyclist
t,would be an arbitrary catalyst.
Or if I see the Priory School
I'd have a really fiery tool.

I could perhaps ask Black Peter
if he has a right crack meter.
Or maybe Charles Augustus Milverton,
Or even an agent of justice, Pinkerton.

If numbers increase the odds from lowly ones
I could then hire Six Napoleons,
or maybe only Three Students.
Then I could claim or plea prudence.

If I found a Golden Pince-Nez,

It could lead to the rhyme I says.
But just like the Missing-Three Quarter,
I don't have it like I ought'er.

I could look in the Abbey Grange,
to get there take a cabby strange.
But just like a Second Stain,
my rhyme, it must be reckoned slain.

Again, I stand, my rhyme is lost.
It must be found at any cost.
When things do look their utmost bleak,
Sherlock Holmes is the one to seek.

Sherlock Holmes and Margate Museum

1st letter

Mitchell Merryweather III,
Curator, Margate Museum of Antiquities
Thanet, Kent, England

7 April, 1898

Dear Mr. Holmes,

My name is Mitchell Merryweather III, and I am the curator of a small museum in the coastal town of Margate, in Thanet, Kent. I am writing to you regarding a mystery of the most profound nature. Historical items of immense value and interest have started disappearing from a secure room in our museum. I am at a loss to explain their disappearance. The strangest aspect of these thefts is that they were predicted, or should I say, threatened, by my grandfather, over a decade ago! It is imperative that these thefts be resolved, or I may lose my job, as well as my lodging.

Our family has lived in Margate for generations and is well-respected. In fact, my grandfather donated the museum building and its contents to the town, along with the curator's cottage. The deed of ownership stipulated that the curator of the museum should live in the adjacent cottage free of charge, as long as he remains in the position of curator. My father lived there during his employment as curator, and when he retired, I took over the position and moved into the cottage. I assumed I would live there for my entire life, but if these thefts are not resolved, my position may be forfeit, as the board wants an answer as to what exactly is going on, particularly since the thefts are directly related to my grandfather's warning. I have been told that if the situation is not resolved, I may be replaced.

I alluded to the fact that my grandfather predicted, or one might say threatened, that these thefts would take place, and I must explain myself. Mitchell Merryweather Senior was a peculiar man, very proud of himself and his accomplishments. He acquired a vast fortune in the shipping industry, and at one time, owned several vessels, the first of which, I am told, he won in a card game, of all things. I myself, cannot conceive of losing something that valuable in a game of cards. The way I heard the story from my father, the gentleman he won the ship from went home, informed his wife what had happened, signed up for the next available voyage to work his way back to owning another ship, but he never returned. He left behind a young daughter whose mother struggled to care for her Feeling remorseful, my grandfather provided generously for the girl while she grew up. She was raised as one of my grandfather's family, but even with his generosity towards her, as she grew older and better understood what had happened, she started feeling anger and animosity towards him regarding what happened to her father. She ran away in the night shortly before her sixteenth birthday, and as far as I know, no one in the family has heard from her since.

Grandfather collected many valuable treasures from around the world. His house, which he had designed and built for himself to elaborate specifications, was often described as a museum while he lived there. As I mentioned, he left his home to the town to become an actual museum, and of course, as a tribute to his success. One of the stipulations, however, was that a certain bust of himself must always be on prominent display on the pedestal in the center of the main foyer. His attending physician stated that on his deathbed, my grandfather promised that when the day came that anything else was ever displayed there, it would vanish in the night. No one gave his threat much thought. After all, he was rather odd, and the town was most grateful for his generous donation, but his image was displayed there for the entire time my father was curator.

When I took over as curator, I set about refreshing some aspects of the museum. My grandfather's bust had occupied the most prominent spot in the whole building, while all sorts of fascinating treasures were relegated to lesser locations. I felt, and the museum board agreed, that my grandfather's statue had been there long enough. Personally, I gave no credence to his threat that his bust must remain there, "or else," and I retired it to the storage attic. Based on the urging of our oldest board member and president, an expert in antiquities himself, I chose to display a valuable Grecian urn there instead. It dated to circa 540 B.C., and was signed by the potter and painter, Tleson. It was quite a unique and special piece. The next morning, the urn was gone, and my grandfather's bust was back in its place. To say the least, the board members and myself were all shocked. We verified that all the locks were still secure, and the local authorities could not find anything amiss, so we are at a loss to determine how the theft was carried out.

The only possible clue was a series of scuff marks on the floor near the pedestal, but they could have been from any number of museum visitors the previous day. The strange thing is that the scuffs only appear near the pedestal; there are no scuff marks going to or from that area. While the police were here, the man who found the marks insisted that upon inspection they seemed to spell out the word "Rose," which was the name of my grandfather's first ship. I looked at them and could not be sure one way or the other. Of course, the scuff marks could be explained easily enough. It could just be that while someone was examining the bust of my grandfather, an impatient child was scuffing the floor in frustration. You have no idea how often we must scrub and polish the floors after a group of young children come tromping through the museum.

The door to the attic storage room was also still locked. As the only one with keys and access to the entire museum, I am deeply concerned that all the evidence points to myself as the perpetrator, but I assure you it was not me. I was in the curator's cottage the entire evening. I did not notice anyone coming or going. How could it possibly have happened?

Not to be intimidated by threats from beyond the grave, I again replaced my grandfather's bust in the storage attic and placed a small but valuable Egyptian statue on the pedestal. Our president suggested the piece himself. It was a basalt head of an official from the middle kingdom, of the 12th or 13th dynasty. He also insisted that we hire a guard to remain outside the museum door for the night, and provided a fellow that he was familiar with, a big strapping brute. However, my efforts were in vain. Once again, when we opened the museum in the morning, the treasure was gone, and my grandfather's bust was back in its place! The guard said he had not heard anything during the night, and nothing could have gotten past him at the door. I did detect the smell of whiskey on the guard, but he proudly stated that he had just had a little nip to keep warm, and that he could put away a full bottle with no ill effects whatsoever. Needless to say, I let him go this morning.

As I stated, I do not believe in curses, or threats from a long-dead individual, even if he is my grandfather. Someone must be behind this, but who? There must be a logical explanation. Of course, I could simply leave the bust in its place, but then the thief would still be at large, and I would still be the prime suspect. I implore your help in this matter. If I do not bring this to resolution, I fear my job and my accommodations are lost.

Sincerely,
Mitchell Merryweather III

2nd letter

Mitchell Merryweather III,
Curator, Margate Museum of Antiquities
Thanet, Kent, England

9 April, 1898

Dear Mr. Holmes,

As I await your reply to my correspondence, things here have gotten even worse than I could have imagined. Since I last wrote you, yet another theft has taken place from the pedestal in the main foyer, and the size of the footprints left behind match my very own! The most valuable item so far has vanished, a Neolithic Chinese jade bi disk from 3000 B.C. And to complicate things even further, the first two items to go missing have been discovered in the office of the museum's president. In addition, a good length of climbing rope has been observed in the office of the board's vice president. How the stolen items got where they did, I have no idea. I assure you; I had nothing to do with it. The board president is denying any knowledge about it, even though he suggested both of the items, and he recommended the guard. The vice president says that everyone knows that he enjoys climbing the local cliffs in his spare time, and that is why the rope was there. Now they are both pointing fingers at each other.

The president is claiming that I put the stolen items in his office, and the vice president feels that I am in cahoots with the president to frame him. This entire affair is getting stranger by the day.

Due to mounting evidence pointing towards me, and now the two original board members, the remaining board member is demanding the resignation of myself, as well as the other two gentlemen, if a satisfactory answer is not provided. As a courtesy to my family and our services to the town over the years, I have been granted a week to provide an explanation. I am hoping that with the additional information that has come to light since my first letter, perhaps you will be able to solve this conundrum. My very livelihood and future is at stake.

That being said, here are further facts that may be pertinent to my situation.

My father's retirement was, in truth, forced upon him by the museum board. The membership of the board has changed over the years, and none of the original board is still present. It all started after the appointment of the newest board member, an older, bald, and bearded gentleman with a strong accent. Even though he was a stranger to the area, he had made a number of significant donations and was unanimously appointed to the position. My father's dismissal was due to differences in opinion as to the running of the museum. He wanted to follow my grandfather's desire to keep the focus on the significance of our family in acquiring the vast majority of the collection. The board, however, based on the urging of the newest member, wanted to change the museum's focus to the area's maritime history and some of the newer nautical acquisitions. When my father refused, they voted to retire him. I took his place as curator, and I am sad to say, that he felt that I betrayed him. He said that if I truly honored grandfather's wishes, I would not have accepted the position, and I would someday regret my decision. When he left, we were not on the best of terms. He did not say where he was going, and I cannot say where he might be now. I have not heard from him since the day that he left. He was tall, slender, like myself, and quite agile, with brown hair and eyes, a rather handsome man. It was often said that I looked much like my father.

He and his brother grew up in the curator's cottage after my grandfather donated his house to become the museum. They did live in the museum house when they were younger, and I am told that they and Lilly, the young daughter of the gentleman he won his ship from, enjoyed playing hide and seek in the endless corridors. Lilly and my uncle were both amazingly good at it and seemed able to truly disappear. My father never did figure out their tricks or win any of their hide and seek games. He did, however, take his history studies and categorizing of the museum's collections very seriously.

My grandfather had always said that he had groomed both his sons to be curators, and carry on the family tradition, but only one could be chosen. On his eighteenth birthday, when my father was named the next curator, his younger brother said that although he felt he was better qualified, he would go to sea and make his own important discoveries. He would someday have a 'big surprise' for everyone. He left and we have not heard from him since. This happened when he was seventeen, long before I was born, so I have never seen him, but I am told he was of average build, clean shaven, and dark-haired.

My grandfather died some years after naming my father the next curator. He was sick for only a short time, although I never knew exactly what his illness was. According to my father, the attending physician was an old acquaintance of my grandfather from his seafaring days, He is the one who said that grandpa's last words were to remember our family's heritage, and never remove his bust from the main pedestal in the foyer, or anything that took its place would vanish. Per his wishes, he was cremated immediately after his death, and his ashes are buried in the museum's gardens, rather prominently of course. Grandfather at the time of his passing, was grey haired, with blue eyes, not very tall, but muscular and still quite alert.

Regarding the museum building itself, I do not have any blueprints of the house. I do recall there being a detailed set of plans that my grandfather kept close watch over, but after he passed away, they were never found. To my knowledge, there are none that still exist.

The main foyer, where the thefts have occurred, is the primary entrance to the building. It is a large octagon in shape, and there are two solid, beautifully carved wooden doors in the front center wall. On the opposite wall is a doorway that leads to the main portion of the museum, and there is a secure, locking door there as well. The bottom portions of the side walls are cherry wood wainscoting, and there are ornate stained-glass windows at the top of each wall of the octagon. I have been told that they depict scenes from my grandfather's travels, and they really are quite lovely. They can be opened to allow fresh air into the foyer, using a long pole. When we found the climbing ropes, we inspected all the exterior windows and found none that seemed to have been forced. However, these windows in the foyer do not lock very well in the first place. They are so high on the wall, we never thought it was that important. The floor is inlaid polished marble, in the form of a compass rose, with the stone pedestal in the exact center. The room is quite tall, with a varnished, wood-beamed ceiling, except for the lowered center portion, which supports a chandelier. With the pedestal in the center, anyone who came into the museum had to go past his image. Grandfather really was quite proud of himself.

After my father left and I took over, I honestly paid no attention to my grandfather's final words. Now, I am beginning to have my regrets regarding that decision. I know there must be a logical answer, and I hope that this offers additional insight into what is happening, as my time is running out. I look forward to hearing from you regarding an answer to my predicament.

Sincerely,
Mitchell Merryweather III

3rd letter

Mitchell Merryweather III,
Curator, Margate Museum of Antiquities
Thanet, Kent, England

14 April, 1898

Dear Mr. Holmes,

It is with great trepidation and concern that I await your reply. I have only two days left to provide an explanation, or I lose everything! The museum's board members are still at odds with each other, with accusations flying back and forth. The guard whom the president hired has vanished, which the vice president says is proof enough to convict him, and the president is claiming that fibers from the vice president's climbing rope are visible in the foyer, so he should be arrested. I myself have not seen any rope fibers, but I have been searching desperately for any possible additional bits of information that could be of use to you.

The most interesting is that flyers have been posted advertising a new museum to be opened on the other side of town. The new "Margate Museum of Historical Treasures" is slated to open this very week. This is the first I have learned of this. I had heard that a large building had recently been purchased by some gentleman from out of the area, and a great deal of work has been going on there, with a large number of deliveries, but I did not know it was to be a museum. That was quite a surprise. The activities going on there have all been quite secretive until the flyers started to appear. It is claiming to offer amazing treasures and antiquities from around the world. What is the likelihood of a second museum of this nature being opened in this location? Could this have anything to do with what is going on? I am quite perplexed.

I recently discovered that our newest board member may also have a seafaring background. He is quite a taciturn fellow, and I really know very little about him. He does not speak a great deal, but the last time we did speak, I happened to notice the tattoo of a compass rose supported by two mermaids on his wrist. It looked somewhat familiar, but I said nothing at the time, since I could not recall exactly where I might have seen it. Then I realized that the compass rose was somewhat similar to the emblem of my grandfather's shipping company. It is not exactly the same, mind you, since it has the two mermaids. But then, I imagine that there are probably a great many sailor tattoos that incorporate a compass. During his entire time on the museum board, whenever he does say something, it has been to strongly promote displays of nautical heritage, so it may be that is just his background. As far as I know, he never knew my grandfather.

Also, in going through the town records of my grandfather's death, I learned more about his attending physician, who was the only one with him at the time of his death and handled the cremation personally. The records stated that the physician was an old acquaintance of my grandfather, which I did know, and that he had even saved my grandfather's life when he was injured at one point in the past, which was news to me. After the funeral and reading of the will, which by the way did not include the doctor, he moved away and has only been seen in the area on rare occasions.

There are also several other very odd items that have occurred in the last few days. This may sound bizarre, but the museum groundskeeper has reported that my grandfather's burial site in the museum garden has been disturbed. It appears as if someone was digging up the grave and then tried to perfectly replace everything that was disturbed. They did a reasonable job of it, but it was still somewhat obvious. Why would anyone disturb the grave of my grandfather, especially at this crucial time in the museum's history?

Secondly, while this next oddity has actually been going on over the last several years, its relevance just occurred to me in regard to the current events. A grey haired, elderly lady, dressed in black, has visited the museum once a month, for several years. She just this week made her monthly visit, and that is when I noticed: she always just stares at the pedestal in the central foyer and murmurs to herself. Over all of the years she has been visiting monthly, she has only observed the pedestal, and nothing more. She appears to be about the age of my father, and looks to be in mourning, as she has a lace veil over her face. No one has ever spoken to her, and she had never said a word to anyone until the day after her most recent visit. She returned and simply asked what had become of the bust that was in the foyer. When I told her it had been retired, she just shook her head and left. I did not know what to think.

One additional oddity is that yesterday, a hunchbacked, white haired, older gentleman was seen on the museum grounds, just looking intensely at the building. He circled the building several times, observing and nodding incessantly. Then upon entering the museum, it seemed like he was only scrutinizing the architecture. I watched him myself, for quite some time, and he paid no attention to any of the exhibits, only the structure of the building. Is it possible that he could be the thief? Why else would someone be examining the features of the museum building in such detail? I can think of no other reason. However, I must say, he had not been seen anywhere in the vicinity of the museum prior to yesterday. If he is the thief, I would think that someone would have noticed him previously, before the first thefts occurred. I am at a loss to explain this new development. Hopefully, it has some bearing on the outcome.

I do hope, with these added details, that I have provided enough information to convince you to help me. As I have stated, my very livelihood and reputation depend upon resolving this predicament.

Sincerely,
Mitchell Merryweather III

4th letter

John H. Watson, M.D.
Margate Post Office
Thanet, Kent, England

15 April, 1898
Afternoon post

Dear Holmes,

I do hope your other critical activity was worth my making the effort to travel up here to Margate. I trust all went well with that case. I know it was important to you. Anyway, I am writing to inform you that I have completed all of your requests regarding the Margate Museum case, exactly per your instructions, as strange as some of them seemed.

My first task on arrival was more than a bit strange even for our adventures, Sherlock. I have to say, that this is the first time I can recall that I have had to dig up a grave! Per your instructions, I waited until well after dark and dug up the grandfather's grave to make sure that there were indeed ashes in the burial urn that was interned there. They were in fact there. Per your suspicions that, if there were no ashes, the thief could have very well been the grandfather, I understand it was necessary, but it was certainly not enjoyable. I tried to replace the ground as neatly as possible, but I did have to leave in a hurry, as someone was coming towards the area. The last thing I want is to be charged with being a grave robber. People would get all kinds of ideas about me. The last thing I need is to be labeled as a Dr. Frankenstein.

The next day I took the measurements that you asked for, using all the precautions that we discussed to avoid recognition. From my inspection, the situation appears to be just as you suspected.

Finally, this morning, I called upon Mr. Merryweather, introduced myself as your associate, and explained to him that while you are already investigating his situation, and are very close to a solution, you were unable to be there in person. He does appear to be an overly excitable gentleman, but then with all that has been going on, I imagine I would not blame him.

When I pointed out that you have also been deeply involved in another equally urgent matter, I thought he was going to faint. However, I must say, when I elucidated to him that his situation grew more intriguing with each additional letter, and you were well on the way to a solution, that did seem to calm him down and get his attention. I told him that you were pleased to take his case, as he had provided a wealth of useful and fascinating information, and I indicated that you already have a theory on exactly how the thefts are taking place.

He was quite pleased to hear that you have a prime suspect, but he was almost beside himself when I identified his father. I explained that his father has a strong motive against the museum board for his dismissal, and to some extent, even against his son, for his perceived betrayal. Revenge can be a great motivator. Mr. Merryweather, Junior was intimately familiar with the building and could have kept a set of keys when he left. In addition, he was the same build as his son, so the footprints that were found could have been from the father.

As you directed me, I told him to be sure and inform the museum board that he had been in communication with Sherlock Holmes, Consulting Detective, and to let them let them know all that I had related to him as well as the identity of the main suspect. I also made sure to let him know that you will have a definitive answer within the day, and only need to visit a nearby village to gather additional evidence to confirm your theory.

Returning to the remainder of your tasks for me, I alerted Mr. Merryweather of the impending delivery of an Egyptian coffin and informed him that it was to be immediately displayed in the entry foyer against a side wall, facing the center pedestal, upright against the wall. Yes, I was emphatic that the coffin was not to be opened under any circumstances. He looked at me rather strangely but said he would obey the instructions regarding the coffin, as well as the small wooden chest that was also to be displayed in the foyer, on the central pedestal. The chest I delivered then and there, and he was quite intrigued with it, especially when I handed him the identification card, describing it as 'The Star of the East, the most valuable and precious jewel from all of India.'

I informed him that the card should be placed directly in front of the sealed chest, and that as soon as the coffin arrives and is set in place he must then close and lock the museum for the night, and beforehand to be sure and inform the board members of the valuable new acquisitions. As you suggested, I mentioned that they will be quite the prize for the museum when it opens in the morning and should help make up for the recent losses. He was quite in a dither but promised to carry out my instructions explicitly.

I did some snooping around the new museum that is to open tomorrow and discovered that they are hoping to put on quite a show. Supposedly the owner is quite knowledgeable in antiquities and ancient history, as well as where to find the best historical treasures. I was not able to learn who it is, but that will be revealed in the morning, when the new museum opens.

One final note is that as you had suspected, the missing hired guard did turn up. I finally found him after I checked enough pubs. It turned out he could not hold his whiskey as well as he thought and had spent every bit of his earnings from his brief guard duty on getting blazing drunk. He had passed out just outside of the Three Goats' Heads pub, and fallen into some bushes, where he slept it off unseen. He would have probably been there longer if I had not noticed him. In truth, it was the odor that led me to him. He smelled like he had been sleeping in a herd of goats.

That is all I have to report. I am sure your suspicions are correct, and we will bring this to a successful conclusion in the morning.

Sincerely,
John H. Watson, M.D.

5th letter

Sherlock Holmes
221-b Baker Street
London, England

16 April, 1898

Dear Mr. Merryweather,

I must apologize for not waiting around to meet you in person this morning after the successful resolution of your predicament, but, as my associate, Dr. Watson had informed you, I had another matter of equal importance to attend to today. You will be pleased to know; the perpetrators have been delivered to the local authorities. They are none other than your grandfather's physician, Dr. William Wentworth, and the museum's newest board member, an acquaintance of his from his time at sea.

I do hope you will pardon my ruse, in naming your father as the prime suspect, but I wanted to throw the real culprits off the trail. When criminals are overconfident, they tend to get rather careless. Your grandfather was indeed well acquainted with his attending physician, who was a ship's surgeon from the Merryweather fleet, but he did not realize the deep-seated jealousy the man held towards him. While Mr. Merryweather, Senior succeeded in his voyages and advanced in wealth and status, Dr. Wentworth remained a ship's doctor and never advanced beyond that position. He had hidden his true feelings from your grandfather, all the while expecting that he might someday receive a just reward for his loyalty. When the doctor treated your grandfather's injury, he expected much more than mere gratitude.

It was while he attended your grandfather during his illness and final days that the opportunity arose. While spending time alone with him, the doctor discovered the museum's blueprints, revealing many secret passages. Realizing what they were, he came up with the plan of the threat to never remove the bust, or the treasures would vanish. The physician was the only person present to record the threat, so it was simple. Then, at some point in the future, when your father, or you did remove the bust, which he was certain would eventually happen, he could bring disgrace to your family by claiming one of you had stolen the museum's treasures.

Your father was so devoted to your grandfather's wishes that he never dreamed of removing the bust during his entire tenure as curator. The doctor grew tired of waiting, so he conspired to place his accomplice on the museum board with donations from his own ocean travels. Once he had him in place, he used his influence to have your father retired. When you were the curator, and you did not feel so strongly about the threat of removing your grandfather's bust, he was able to put his plan into effect, utilizing the hidden passageways.

As you had stated, Mr. Merryweather, Senior was a very peculiar fellow. What he wanted these secret passages for originally, we may never know. Your uncle had discovered them as a child. That is how he was able to disappear and reappear during those games of hide and seek. So did Lilly, the daughter of the gentleman he won his first ship from in that fateful card game.

The secret passages are how Dr. Wentworth had access to the locked foyer, as well as the storage attic to retrieve the bust and replace it on the pedestal. I was able to deduce the presence of secret passageways and confirmed my suspicions through clandestine observation of the inside and outside of the museum. I easily determined how the thefts were taking place, and only needed to lay a trap to catch the one responsible. At that point there were still several possible suspects. It could also have been your uncle or Lilly who was behind the thefts. They both had strong motives.

Of course, the white haired, hunchbacked gentleman that you had noticed, was my associate, Dr. Watson. I could not allow for him to be recognized, because I did not want to let anyone know that I was already deeply involved in your case and scare off the perpetrators. I suspected that more than one person was involved, since the threat of removing the bust of your grandfather on the one hand, and the knowledge of the secret passages on the other, had to come from a hidden source behind the newest board member, who was an unknown, unfamiliar to everyone in your family. No had thought to connect him to the doctor.

The area above the ceiling chandelier, over the pedestal, concealed a secret entryway into the foyer. It was a rope that was lowered to access the treasures, and the scuff marks that were found are an entirely different matter which I will explain momentarily. That is how he stole the treasures and replaced them with the bust of your grandfather. The doctor, despite his age, is still quite agile and muscular from his days at sea.

I thought the newest board member was his source of information, and when you informed the board of the great treasure that was just waiting in the foyer, I knew he would inform his leader, and the thief would not be able to resist the bait. As he came again last night, he saw the label on the chest and could not help but open it to see the priceless jewel. When he did, he was so focused on what he expected to find, he never saw me in back of him. I was hiding inside the Egyptian coffin the whole time and witnessed the entire proceedings. Once I had him securely restrained, he confessed to everything, including leaving footprints that matched yours. Using his access, he stole a spare set of your shoes while you were distracted with everything that was going on. I had my associate Dr. Watson, along with the local constables apprehend his accomplice, and they are now both behind bars.

There are a few additional matters that I would like to elaborate on. Should you decide to pay a visit to the new museum that is opening today, you will see that the owner and manager is your long-vanished uncle. You indicated in your letter that he felt he was the more qualified curator, so he set out to prove it by collecting even greater treasures and artifacts and opening an even better museum in your own backyard, so to speak. It is his 'big surprise.' While this may create a challenge to you, he had nothing to do with the robberies.

One item I do need to explain is that the disturbance to your grandfather's grave was done on my behalf. I had to make absolutely sure that his ashes really were buried there, and that he was not perpetuating an elaborate hoax. The grave's disturbance would have been undetected, but my associate was interrupted and had to leave rather quickly.

The final matter is a bit sadder. Using my contacts, and network of eyes and ears, I was able to track down the mysterious lady in black. While your grandfather showed the Lilly every kindness he could, she grew resentful towards him regarding the loss of her father. .

She felt he was responsible and had left in anger. When I spoke to her, she said that, over the years, having witnessed numerous others destroying their lives by gambling away fortunes, she realized it was her father's fault, and not your grandfather's. She came back to apologize, but he had already passed on. Since that time, she had returned monthly to pay her respects to his memory, the bust in the foyer. It was she that left the scuff marks next to the pedestal that day.

Now that the mystery is solved, and your position is safe, I wish you continued success in your curatorship, and I leave it up to you to decide where to place the bust of your grandfather.

Sincerely,
Sherlock Holmes
Consulting Detective

Sherlock Holmes Returns the Missing Rhyme

Once more I sat with pen in hand,
Before my typewriter so grand.
Engaged deep in the poet's craft.
Why? don't ask, I must be daft.

Again, a rhyme was being vexing.
Finding it was most perplexing.
When suddenly upon my door,
There came a rap, and then one more.

"Now who could that be?" I declared.
And opened it, just somewhat scared.
Well, I'll be, and rattle my bones,
If it isn't the famous Sherlock Holmes.

"What are you doing here?" I said.
He answered, "This is the place that I was led.
You're looking for a rhyme, I know.
All the clues do tell me so.

At first it was a foggy haze,
But then, came it like a Silver Blaze.
Delivered in a Cardboard Box
Disguised as clever as a fox.

To miss it sure would be disgrace
Almost like a Yellow Face.
I knew that you could make it work,
As clear as a Stockbroker's Clerk.

Or smooth as any sailing yacht,
Just like the famous Gloria Scott"
I analyzed. (It is habitual.)
Twas easy as the Musgrave Ritual.

I was quite quick; I was on fire.
As slick as any Reigate Squire.
In color, and hue, it looked tan,
More so than a Crooked Man.

With clues I am the Precedent facient
More often than the Resident Patient"
First, I saw a meek conservator,
and then did find a Greek Interpreter.

Twas obvious as a claval, meaty,
Clearer than a Naval Treaty.
The steps to you, why, I did Gobble 'em
Quicker than The Final Problem.

So here at last, is your lost rhyme,
The best detective, surly I am,
Known by all, why even gnomes,
I am the famous Sherlock Holmes.

Sherlock Holmes and The Phantom Highwayman

1st letter

Robert Collingsly
Collingsly Cartage & Transport
Dover, East Kent, England

Dear Mr. Holmes,

Your reputation for the highest level of deduction, and reaching logical, rational conclusions is unequalled, and as such, I must call upon you about a certain matter at hand. I am at my wits end. It appears that my coaches are being robbed by a spectral being, or to put it bluntly, the ghost of my brother is robbing me.

Some years ago, my brother and I started a small transport company to transfer goods by carriage. We began with one solidly built coach and soon expanded to several. We hired only the most honest and reliable drivers. Our reputation for timely delivery and secure transport of goods, brought us several lucrative contracts, and we became quite successful.

I was in charge of the business aspect of things, while my brother designed, and along with our head carpenter, built the coaches we used. My brother, Charles, had always been an inventor and tinkerer, and to be quite frank, was easily distracted by his interest in scientific, and other less than practical curiosities. He had even wanted me to invest money into a ludicrous idea regarding communication with the spirit world. Our lead carpenter had come up with that rather preposterous scheme, and convinced Charles to work on it with him. He was quite certain had a designed a device that would work, and just needed more funds, and my brother's help to complete it. Charles would routinely get sidetracked and miss deadlines for the completion of new carriages. I gave him several warnings, but this finally led to me dismissing him from the company. When he left, he swore I would be sorry, for he said, he had designed a theft proof coach that he was about to unveil to me, and now, I would never realize the advantage of it.

Then, just after his termination, he returned to our stable, took one of our coaches, drove it to a bluff overlooking the sea, unhitched the horses, climbed into the driver's seat, released the brake, let it roll off the cliff and fall into the waves, and rocks below. The one witness, who saw the event from a distance, said he heard a voice that hollered something about returning from the grave to exact his revenge. The surrounding beaches and coast were searched, but his body was never found. I feel that I am horribly to blame.

That brings me to the current situation. One of my company's business contracts involves the transportation of chests of payroll funds, along the same route that my brother took the day of his death. On two occasions, the coaches have been robbed by an unworldly spectral being, if you will, a phantom highwayman. The drivers, both honest, sober, and reliable men, swear that it was the ghost of my brother, and have refused to drive that route any longer. There is no other route available, and the firm whose funds have twice been stolen has threatened to terminate their business with me unless this matter is resolved. That is why I am turning to you. I am certain you can find a logical explanation to this and bring this matter to a successful conclusion.

In both cases, the driver and his assistant were delivering a small, locked chest with the payroll funds for a mid-sized company. The trunk was placed inside the coach, and the doors were locked. When they neared a wooded area in close proximity to the location of my brother's death, a heavy fog or smoke obscured the path. The driver slowed the carriage, and then both the driver and the assistant saw, in the fog, a ghostly image of my brother wearing a hooded cape and pointing at them with his left hand. While his lips never actually moved, they heard the words, "You will pay!" uttered twice, then the image vanished, and the fog cleared. When the coach arrived at its destination, and the door was unlocked, the chest had vanished. It was nowhere to be found. I ask you; how could it disappear from inside a locked carriage? No one had approached or opened the coach from the time the chest was loaded, until it arrived. I implore your aid, Mr. Holmes. If there is any other information I can provide, I will do so at once. I find myself getting quite sick over this situation. I anxiously await your reply.

Sincerely,
Robert Collingsly

2nd letter

Sherlock Holmes
221-b Baker Street
London, England

Dear Mr. Collingsly,

I offer you my condolences on the passing of your brother, that is, if he has indeed passed away. It sounds like that fact is not entirely certain, and the lack of a body is quite significant in this situation. I read your letter with interest and curiosity and have decided to accept your case.

Firstly, I would like to assure you, that you are not being robbed by ghosts. Even if there were such a thing as a ghost, it would have no need of physical currency. The question that remains then, is to discover who is behind these thefts, and how they are being perpetrated. I already have a theory, but I require additional information, prior to reaching a definitive conclusion.

You mentioned there being a witness to your brother's death. What time did the incident occur? Who was present at the time it happened? How physically close was the person to the cliff, and what were they doing there at that time? Did the witness have an unobstructed view?
Did the fog, or smoke that accompanied the ghost, have any particular type of odor?

Also, what information can you provide on the driver's assistant? You stated that there was one, present in each case, but did not provide any further details.

Tell me more, if you can, about the head carpenter that was working with your brother. Is he still with your firm? Where was he at the time of your brother's passing, and also, when the robberies occurred?

Do you have any blueprints for the coaches your brother designed and built, specifically, the one that was robbed? Did it have any special or unusual features? When the coach was returned to your facility after the robberies, who had access to it? Was it left unattended and unsecured at any point?

When is the next scheduled delivery of a payroll funds chest? We may need to make some additional arrangements for that delivery.

One final question. Was your brother right or left-handed?

I await your reply and look forward to bringing this matter to a successful and rational conclusion. I assure you; the answer will not be found in the realm of the supernatural.

Sincerely,
Sherlock Holmes
Consulting Detective

3rd letter

Robert Collingsly
Collingsly Cartage & Transport
Dover, East Kent, England

Dear Mr. Holmes,

I can not thank you enough for accepting this case. I shall endeavor to provide you the answers to your queries in hopes that your initial suspicions are correct, and that this matter can be laid to rest. Each day that this goes on, I find myself feeling weaker and sicker. My daily cup of chamomile tea provides little relief.

Regarding the witness, the only person present was Mark Brightman, the head carpenter who worked along side my brother. He is a tinkerer also, and the two of them were quite often working late in our carriage shop on one odd device or another. Some of their projects seemed a bit unusual, and I was skeptical about their usefulness to our coaches. They often exchanged correspondence with other scientists and inventors. (Many times, on subjects which had nothing to do with coach building, mind you.) The most recent letters that I saw come across his desk were from a Henry Morton, of America.

After my brother was dismissed, he was quite despondent and wanted to continue working in our firm's shop on his own. However, we had coaches to build to meet the increased business demand and could not spare the space or time, so I refused his request.

Then one evening, at approximately 7:00 pm, I was told, he returned to our stable, hitched up one of our coaches, and drove it to the shore road, five-mile marker. That is the place he perished. Mr. Brightman, who was the only employee on the premises at the time, had seen him leaving, and saddled up a horse to go after him. By the time had he arrived, my brother had already set the horses loose, released the brake, and was rolling towards the cliff. Mr. Brightman has stated, he had an unobstructed view from a reasonable distance. He tried to call out to my brother, but it was no use. The carpenter was quite distraught that he had not arrived in time to stop my brother. He did climb down a pathway to the beach but only found the wreckage of the coach.

He has since volunteered to ride as assistant on any delivery trips that take that route, apparently, in hopes of communicating with the spirit of my brother. I take no stock in communication with the spirit realm, but we do need an assistant driver, and he is the only one who wants to take the position for these deliveries.

Regarding the mysterious fog that appeared on both occasions, one of the drivers did report an odd odor to it, something that he had noticed once before, but could not recall where.

In investigating the answer to your question pertaining to plans for the coaches, while I found blueprints for our earlier coach designs, I have not found any plans for our newest coach, the one that is used for the deliveries of the money chests. The head carpenter says that my brother never made any, he just worked from an idea in his head and directed the construction personally. It is of heavier construction and a bit taller than our earlier designs, and also has two additional break levers. I was told it is to resist forced entry, but beyond that, it seems rather normal to me.

After the thefts had been discovered, the coach was returned to our stables, cleaned, and locked up. The only ones with the keys are myself and Mr. Brightman. He tends to work quite late at times, but throughout all this he has been quite diligent, and has completed his work assignments per the schedule. He has even taken over making my daily tea in the morning.

I am not sure why you would want to know, but my brother was right-handed.

Our next payroll funds delivery is in two days, at 8:00 am, and the client has stated, if this delivery is not successful, they will terminate their contact with us. I fully understand their position. Whether or not a ghost is behind this, we must resolve this matter. I am at your disposal and do hope you have come to a positive conclusion.

Sincerely,
Robert Collingsly

4th letter

Sherlock Holmes
221-b Baker Street
London, England

Dear Mr. Collingsly,

I am now quite confident in my conclusion regarding your situation. I believe that your phantom highwayman predicament, as well as, your mysterious illness, will soon be resolved. All that remains now, is to move forward with your next payroll funds delivery as scheduled. Be certain to utilize the same coach as has been used previously. Also, Mr. Brightman may continue in his position as driver's assistant. I have one additional note regarding your lead carpenter; during the course of my investigations, I discovered that Mr. Brightman's mother passed away recently. Were you aware of this? Since your regular drivers are refusing to drive the Shore Road route, I have a found a coach driver who Is not concerned with ghosts and has agreed to take their place. He will be at your stables at the prescribed time and will have in his possession a unique device that looks like a large airgun. Do not be concerned, it is a part of my plan. It is imperative that you utilize the driver I am sending to you.

I have one final instruction, and that is, until this is resolved, avoid drinking your morning tea. Accept it as usual, but do not drink it. Do not mention our correspondence, or my plan to anyone in your firm. I shall provide the answers and a logical resolution to you soon.

Sincerely,
Sherlock, Holmes

5th letter,

Sherlock Holmes
221-b Baker Street
London, England

Dear Mr. Collingsly,

I am pleased to have this letter delivered to you via the very hand of your brother, who has managed to return from the dead. The attempted coach robbery played out exactly as I predicted, and your phantom highwayman, who was not the ghost of your brother, nor any other ghost, is in the hands of authorities. The perpetrator of the carriage thefts, the supposed death of your brother, and your mysterious illness was your lead carpenter, Mr. Brightman. I will say, he was motivated by the death of his mother, and his attempts to communicate with her, but that does not excuse his actions.

He had convinced your brother to work on a device to try and reach her in the spirit world, and with the help of Charles, he thought he could could actually do so. However, when his funds were exhausted, and your brother was dismissed, he was desperate, and he came up with a scheme to acquire the funds and ensure your brothers continued help. It was a multi-layered plot that involved him kidnapping your brother, with himself being the only witness to tell the story, that he saw Charles taking the coach and running it off the cliff to his death. Once he held Charles as a prisoner, he persuaded him to continue working on the spirit communication device by slipping a small amount of poison in your tea every day, and promising to stop, only when the device was finished. Your brother was working desperately on it, only to get him to stop poisoning you.

Mr. Brightman had come up with a plan to steal the funds he needed by creating the phantom highwayman. He took a daguerreotype of your brother, and using an opaque projector similar to the megascope that was invented by the French scientist, Jacques Charles, he projected the image on an artificial fog of the type that is used in the Globe Theater, for stage effects. You mentioned him receiving correspondence from Henry Morton of America. Mr. Morton is noted for his work on opaque projectors. The phantom highwayman provided an alibi and a distraction to the drivers, but he still had to get his hands on the chest of money. To do that he he used your brother's theft-proof coach, that he had built, but not yet shown to you or anyone else. Your lead carpenter, who had helped build it, was the only person familiar with it.

The design was ingenious actually. When you mentioned it was taller than the others and had two additional break levers, I at once suspected a trap door to a false bottom in the coach. It could be activated by the levers from the forward seat. The driver was so distracted and scared by the phantom, he never noticed Mr. Brightman pulling the lever to drop the chest into the false bottom of the coach. When it arrived at its destination, the chest had vanished from a locked coach. Since he had the keys to the stable, and typically worked late, after the coach had been returned, he could remove the chest at his leisure. He had an accomplice operating the fog machine near the place were your brother supposedly died, so the setup was perfect.

But there were several clues that gave him away. Your brother was right-handed, but his image was pointing with his left hand. That indicated that he was forced to pose for the image. There was the correspondence from Henry

Morton on projectors, and the distinctive smell of the mysterious fog. I suspected his ruse, and using a disguise, I was your replacement driver today. The unusual gun I brought with me, was a compressed air device that disrupted the fog as well as the image of the ghost. I was able to take him by surprise when he tried to drop the chest into the false bottom. When he realized his game was over, he confessed to everything, and then led me to where your brother was being held prisoner. Mr. Brightman was truly crushed when he realized he would never be able to finish his communication device to talk to his deceased mother.

The remaining funds have been returned to the company from which they were stolen, and your brother is alive and well, and from what he said, is anxious to return to his former position, if possible. I am sure after his adventure as a phantom highwayman, he will be more focused on his work, so I would hope that his getting his job back has more than just a ghost of a chance.

Sincerely,
Sherlock Holmes
Consulting Detective

A Modern Detectologist
(That's "Consulting Detective")
(With a tip of the hat to Gilbert and Sullivan)

I am the very model of a modern Detectologist
I've information useful to most any criminologist.
I know the crooks of England and I quote their deeds historical
from Ripper Jack to Twisted Lip in order catagorical;

I'm very well acquainted too, with matters of all kinds of dirt
and any stain that one might find on any different kind of shirt
About footprints, you know I'm teeming with a lot o' news
With many cheerful facts about any street that I might choose

I'm very good at seeing clues, even those invisible
I know the scientific names of anything divisible
In short in matters pertinent to any criminologist
I am the very model of a modern Detectologist.
That's "Consulting Detective", in fact.

I know our ancient history, that is full of every kind of crook
I can name them all with out the use of any book
I quote the names of tobaccos from just the very smallest ash,
no matter where or when the thief may have chose to hide his
stash

I can tell from just a single crumb, what a hoodlum had for
lunch.
It is a scientific fact and not a random guess, or hunch.
Then I can tell from just a bit of chalk that you won't invest in a
stock,
even if it came to you as a surprise or a great shock

Then I can write in secret code, made up of little dancing men,
about a crime in great detail, exactly where, and why, and
when.
In short in matters pertinent to any criminologist

I am the very model of a modern Detectologist
That's "Consulting Detective", by the way.

In fact, when I do know by sight, which house has a secret room,
it will be the downfall and the criminal's final, ending doom.
When such affairs, as tricks and traps happen to come into play
There is no one else who can quite hope to seize the day

When I have learnt what progress has been made in modern Chemistry
When I know more of firearms and any types of weaponry
In short, when I've a smattering of knowledge on all types of dust,
You'll say a better Detectologist has never quite been so robust.

For my logical deduction, though I'm thorough and exemplary
my conclusions are with out doubt really quite peremptory
but, still in matters pertinent to any criminologist
I am the very model of a modern Detectologist.
That's "Consulting Detective", of course.

Sherlock Holmes and the Three Sisters

1st Letter

Miss Beryl Buckland
Islip, Oxfordshire, England
1 July, 1887

Dear Mr. Holmes,

Having read about your crime solving exploits which indicate uncanny abilities in observation, deduction, and logic, I have determined that you are the only possible person who can prevent a crime, that I believe, is about to happen.

My name is Miss Beryl Buckland, eldest daughter of the geologist, William Buckland, and his wife, Mary Morland, aka Mrs. William Buckland, who was also a noted geologist, working at the Oxford Museum. I have two younger sisters, twins, Miss Amber, and Miss Amethyst. After our parents had passed on, we three inherited their estate home, along with an exceptionally large accumulation of fossils and various geological specimens. We were told, that when we finished their work of classifying and cataloguing the entire collection, we would receive a great reward, but were not told what it would be, nor from whom it would come. It was rumored that during one of their field expeditions, they had uncovered a rare and valuable gem of some sort, but had kept it well hidden, even denying its existence. "They were scientists pure and simple," they would say. Their treasure was the knowledge they learned through their research and discovery. Yet still, the rumor persisted.

In addition to my sisters and and myself, the only other person living at our home is our caretaker, James. He brings the boxes of specimens to the sorting room and takes care of regular chores around the property.

I have been diligently working on the collection for a number of years, (the collection really is quite considerable.) almost since since their passing, and in truth, I do enjoy it. It is quite fascinating and a pleasant diversion from the outside world. My sisters on the other hand are another story. Although they are twins, and identical in appearance, they could not be more different in personality.

Miss Amber is quite and withdrawn; one would almost say antisocial. She cares nothing for her appearance, or outside interests. She regularly helps me in the cataloging and classification of the collection and then spends her all her free time in pouring over our parent's journals and diaries from their travels. She has said nothing about what she has found in the journals, just that it is fascinating, and keeps her occupied.

Miss Amethyst, however, is more interested in the latest fashions and socializing with other ladies, and men in town. In the past, when we did convince her to help with the collection, she had rushed through it with little care or concern. That is, however, until recently. Lately she has been paying much closer attention our work on the collection. It is as if she is looking for something specific. She will spend hours going through the material, and then suddenly drop everything, grab her purse, and rush off saying she almost forgot about a meeting, or some such thing. When she returns, she just goes back to the cataloging in great detail. Her change in behavior began when she started seeing a gentleman who had previously traveled with our parents on several of their collecting trips. They met at a social function, spent quite a bit of time together, and then suddenly, she started paying much more attention to helping me sort and catalogue everything. She has even invited him over to help with her efforts, occasionally.

I suspect that this gentleman may be giving her instructions on what clues in the collection to look for. And then, when she finds something that may be pertinent, she rushes off to report and then returns with new directions. Since he worked with our parents, he may have some knowledge about the rumored valuable find, and its connection to the mysterious reward that was promised us when work on the collection was completed. I believe the two of them are trying to secretly discover whatever it is and steal it when they do. I know that it may seem poor of me to suspect my very own sister, but her actions seem to point in that direction. We must stop this crime before it happens. Is there any way you can help? I am truly beside myself with concern. I am certain, that if you can only pay a visit, you would be able to solve everything. But I must ask you, please do not say that I requested your assistance. That would seem odd to my sisters, I am sure. I am certain you could come up with some acceptable reason for visiting.

I look forward to your reply, and even more, your resolving this situation.

Sincerely,
Miss Beryl Buckland

2nd letter

Miss Amber Buckland
Islip, Oxfordshire, England
2 July, 1887

Dear Mr. Holmes,

Your reputation for perception, logic, and deduction precedes you, and as such I feel that I can turn to you with my rather peculiar situation.

My name is Miss Amber Buckland, daughter of the well-known geologist, William Buckland, who wrote the very first description of a dinosaur, the Megelasaurous, and won the the Copley medal for his work at Kirkdale Cave. My mother, Mary Morland, later, Mrs. William Buckland, was also a noted geologist, who worked on fossils at the Oxford Museum. I have one older sister, Miss Beryl, and my twin sister, Miss Amethyst. Our parents have both passed on, and my sisters and I inherited their estate home, which came with an extensive accumulation of fossils and geological specimens. Besides ourselves, there is a caretaker who lives in the servant's wing just down the hallway from our rooms and helps us in moving the heavy boxes of minerals and fossils to the room where we sort and catalogue them.

In addition, to the geological specimens, they also left behind their expedition diaries. I have spent most of my free time reading and rereading them since they passed away. When I do, it is as if they are right there in the room, talking to me, telling me their secrets. I can even hear their voices at times telling me things.

My father passed away first, due to complications from a neck injury years earlier. My mother continued his work illustrating the specimens and adding to the collection, and then she passed away a year later. In the will that gave us the house, and their estate in equal shares, we were told, that when we finished their work of classifying and cataloguing the entire collection, we would receive some sort of significant reward. However, we were never told what it would be, nor where, exactly it would come from. There was a brief rumor that on one of their field expeditions, they had discovered a very rare and valuable gemstone of some sort, and not recorded it, but that is utter nonsense, as my parents were professional scientists. My father was also a Theologian, and the Dean of Westminster. There is no reason he would not have recorded such a find. It would have been against his very principles.

Yet, there seems to be something very strange going on. My older sister, I am sure, believes in the hidden treasure rumors, as she has spent an inordinate amount of time involved in sorting and cataloging the collection. Yes, I too, have spent a great amount of time working in the collection, and the expedition diaries, but that is my life. I have no interest in socializing or meeting anyone. We are reasonably well off from our parent's estate, and I have no need of anyone else, (except of course, your services to solve this conundrum.) But she is the eldest, and she is attractive, well versed in the sciences, she has had gentleman callers, I could go on, but I think you understand. I believe she is infatuated by the idea of some great treasure, and I fear she will stop at nothing to obtain it, weather it exists or not.

My twin sister, Miss Amethyst, is extremely outgoing and fashion minded, and as of recently has a gentleman friend who she is spending time with. He had accompanied our parents on several of their field expeditions, and I believe his influence may be why she has shown a renewed interest in working on the collection. Since making his acquaintance, she has taken to working diligently for hours, and then running off unexpectedly, only to return to working as if nothing has happened. I believe she is providing him scientific information on certain items, and possibly even sneaking samples out to him. He has been writing articles, and technical papers, and has made several minor references to specimens in our parent's collection. He seems to be utilizing some of their finds in his writing. He does briefly mention their source, but like many scientists who purchase specimens from amateur collectors, and then take credit for making them known, I think his motives are self serving.

Returning to my sister, Beryl, she is constantly watching Miss Amethyst when she is working with the collection. It is as if she suspects that Miss Amethyst and her beau are trying to steal something really important. I have seen her go through the items Amethyst has worked on, just to see if something may be missing. And I have even observed Beryl hiding specific specimens. The last time Miss Amethyst tried to leave suddenly, Beryl was almost violent with her, demanding she explain herself.

I understand, the information I have provided is vague, and minimal, but can you provide any answers to what is going on here? Perhaps if you examined things in person, you could find an answer before something terrible happens. Of course, you can not say that I invited you. That would seem improper. Just mention that you have heard of our work, express an interest the fossils, and Beryl would be happy to show them to you.

I await your reply,
Sincerely Miss Amber Buckland

3rd letter

Miss Amethyst Buckland
Islip, Oxfordshire, England
3 July, 1887

Dear Mr. Holmes,

I am writing to you regarding a number of very odd
occurrences in our household. I fear if something is not
done soon, a tragic event may befall us. From what I have
read and heard, about you, there is no-one, beyond yourself
who can see the unseen, and deduce exactly what is going
on.

My name is Miss Amethyst Buckland. I have an older
sister, Miss Beryl, and a twin sister, Miss Amber. Our
parents were both well know geologists and left us a vast
accumulation of fossils and mineral specimens, along with
their estate when they passed away. The strangest part of
their will was the request to catalog and classify their entire
collection, with the assurance of a great reward when the
work was completed. Perhaps it was their way of making
sure something useful would be done with the mounds of
unsorted fossils and specimens left behind when they
passed away. They were quite dedicated to their work. To
give you an example, when they got married, their
honeymoon was a year long field expedition, collecting
rocks and fossils. Can you even imagine that? That is not
what I would call a honeymoon!

I will be honest with you, I initially had truly little interest
in the working on the collection, even with our caretaker's
help, moving all the items from the storage areas to the

sorting room. However, I recently made the acquaintance of a handsome gentleman, Roger Rathmore, who worked with my parents on some of their field expeditions. I realized, that with a little help, he could become almost as well known, and respected as my parents were, and land a well-paid position in academics or the sciences. And I am in a convenient place to give him that help, if you understand what I am saying. He has been visiting us, to help me with my efforts. He even stays over in the guest room when necessary.

Our parents left the three of us reasonably well off, but it can only last for so long. Both of my sisters are infatuated with sorting and cataloging the collection, and show no interest in getting married, so they will be relying on our parent's estate well into the future. I intend to be married to a respected and well compensated husband, and I am assisting my intended, by making available interesting pieces from the collection, to author papers on. There are so many specimens, I cannot see what difference removing one or two would make, and I do return them, when he is finished writing papers on them.

However, in the beginning of this letter, I referred to several odd occurrences and an impending tragic event. During one of our parent's expeditions, there was a rumor of a valuable piece that was never reported. The rumor was vehemently denied by them, but I am certain my oldest sister firmly believes it and feels that the completing the cataloging of the collection will lead to it, the promised, "great reward". As we get closer to completion, she has become positively consumed by that idea. Her behavior lately has been becoming quite erratic. I believe she thinks I intend to steal this nonexistent treasure. She is watching me like a hawk and has even gotten almost violent when I have to leave to take care of other things. If someone does not stop her, she may do something that could very well endanger my life.

Even more concerning is my twin sister Miss Amber. She has no social life at all, and when she is not sorting and classify the collection, she is pouring over our parent's diaries from their field expeditions. At times, I have even overheard her, with one of them in her hand, talking to our parents. Not just wishful reminiscing but having conversations. It is one sided of course, but she carries on like they are actually right there speaking to her. Just the other day I overheard her reading from the diaries, reciting some lines in verse. It went something like,
"Knowledge is the greatest treasure,
important, yes beyond all measure,
but the hidden helping hand,
reveals the final answer grand."

And then she said, "Yes, yes, it does make sense, "and continued,
"Time immortal soon will tell,
If you've done your job quite well.
Or if you are weak and frail
Then you three will surely fail."

However, if you do persist
And temptations do resist,
Your names forever you will find
Will be eternally enshrined."

That sounds like total nonsense to me. I feel she may be losing her sanity. Perhaps you and your associate, Doctor Watson could talk to her and make some recommendations. She may need to be put in a special place if you know what I mean.

As you can see by my observations, it is urgent that you come by to visit us, but please do not mention that I asked you to. Perhaps you can just say that you have heard of our parents' vast collection and wanted to view it. We do occasionally receive requests of that nature.

I await your reply,
Sincerely,
Miss Amethyst Buckland

4th letter

John Watson, M.D.
Islip, Oxfordshire, England
4 July, 1887

Afternoon Post

Dear Holmes,

I realize you are quite occupied at the moment, but I do not know how you talk me into these things. I really do enjoy accompanying you on your cases. Some are positively fascinating, but this one is truly bizarre. When you handed me the three letters that you received from the three Buckland sisters, over a three-day period, I thought it was just for my amusements before you tossed them into the fireplace. I never dreamed you would be sending me here to their home, with a list of specific observations to make. I do not see how you could have read anything significant in their letters. To me, one of them is just wasting her time on an imagined treasure hunt, while the third is planning out a comfortable future by paving the way for her intended, husband's success; and the second is just living in a fantasy world, conversing with her deceased parents.

I did use the story you made up, that I was in the vicinity on medical business, and had heard of the amazing collection of fossils and minerals that their famous parents had left behind. When I mentioned an interest in coprolites, they more than welcomed me into their house. But really, Holmes, fossilized dinosaur dung? How you even knew that fossilized dinosaur dung is called coprolites is beyond me. Couldn't you think of anything else for me to ask about? As it turned out, you were spot on. Their parents left them a table with coprolites inlaid into the surface. Can you believe that? From what I was told by his daughters, William Buckland was quite eccentric. He sometimes delivered lectures on horseback. When lecturing indoors, he would cavort in front of his class imitating the dinosaurs he was talking about, and he had even claimed to have eaten his way through the entire animal kingdom, including mole, blue-fly, and crocodile. He was a very strange one.

I will say, it was brilliant to have me ask about how they move all the heavy pieces about. When they mentioned that the caretaker does all the heavy lifting, I expressed concern for his health and offered to check his heart. Of course, they were most appreciative and gave me time to talk with him during the exam.

Returning to the three sisters, that is what seemed odd. At first, I did not notice any animosity similar to what was referenced in the letters. When I arrived, I saw that each one of them seemed to be interested in what they, themselves were doing. They only called their caretaker, James, when they need him to move boxes. As I mentioned, I did get to speak to him as you requested. Interestingly, he seemed to express the very same concerns that were mentioned in the letters, especially, the motives of Miss Amethyst's gentleman friend. James does not trust him at all. It seems that Roger, Miss Amethyst's gentleman friend, has been visiting quite often to help her in her efforts. And when he is not here, she leaves, and runs off, quite unexpectedly, and then returns to her sorting without saying a word. Roger did pay a visit while I was there. I spoke with him briefly, and he went on about what a treasure trove the collection was. He said he could spend a lifetime examining the specimens. He mentioned that he is always looking for new examples to write about. I offered to let him know if I found any, and he enthusiastically wrote down his address for me.

I learned that James was also one of their parent's expedition team members for several years. He said that he does his job out of respect for his former employers, continuing to work as a caretaker/ground's keeper, for their daughters. I asked, what will happen when they finish cataloging the collection. He just replied that his job will be much easier, without all the boxes to move. I also asked him what happens if they do not finish the job of classifying everything. He just nodded, and said, "Indeed, what happens then?", and did not say anything more on that subject.

Per your request, I also observed his quarters while we were talking. His room is down the hall, next to the guest room, not far from Miss Amber's. As you suspected, there was a safe, in his room, tucked away in a corner. There was a coat on top of it, that looked like it had been hastily thrown over it when he answered the door, but it was still slightly visible. He did glance at it several times during our conversation but said nothing about it. The other two sister's rooms are further down the hallway going towards the large ball room that was converted to a storage area, followed by the library room which is where they do the sorting and classifying. I did have an opportunity to just glance in the guest room. It seemed normal enough, but I noticed, partially hidden under a shawl, a tube of some sort going into the wall. I am not certain what that was for. It reminded me of a speaking tube that was used to call servants, years ago. There is also an entire barn outside that was used for storage of specimens.

Just after I finished his medical exam, and was perusing the collection, which by the way, looks almost complete, things got even stranger. Miss Beryl claimed she caught Miss Amethyst trying to steal valuable specimens. James had mentioned to Beryl that he thought he saw her putting pieces in her purse. She had found some valuable pieces in Miss Amethyst's bag, while her sister said she knew nothing about them. Then Miss Amber came running up to me saying she had discovered a handgun in Miss Beryl's desk and feared for her sister's life. She said her parents had told her to look for it there, that their lives were in danger. Miss Beryl was shocked and said she had never seen it before in her life, that Miss Amber was delusional. And finally, Miss Amethyst came to me and said she had heard Miss Amber having conversations with herself again, something about a gun, and that she really felt she should be removed and put in a safe place.

I am not sure what to make of it all. I did manage to get them settled down and said that I was sure there was a logical explanation, that it just needed to be found. If they had had their way, two of them would have been locked in jail, while the third would have been put in an institution. Fortunately, they listened to reason, and my assurance that I knew an expert who could quickly resolve the entire situation. I confiscated the gun and told them you would have an answer forthcoming, and to just be patient for a while. I do hope you have an answer to this tangled mess.

I did manage to get the samples of everyone's handwriting, which took some very clever work on my part. They are included in this letter. I am not sure what you will make of all this, but I know you have an answer in mind. I look forward to hearing it.

Sincerely,
John Watson, M.D.

5th letter

Sherlock Holmes, Consulting Detective
Fifth letter
221-b Baker Street
London, England

4, July, 1887

Dear Miss: Beryl, Amber, and Amethyst,

My name is Sherlock Holmes, Consulting Detective, and I do believe that this is the first time in my career, that I am writing to my client, or should I say clients, to explain the resolution of a case, prior to them even knowing that there was a case to be solved, or that they were in fact my clients.

I recently received three individual letters, each one claiming to be from one of you, requesting my help in solving various odd occurrences in your home, regarding a large fossil and mineral collection, and a rumored great treasure.

From the letters, I am familiar with your family history, and your parent's accomplishments in geology and paleontology, and particularly the rumored treasure and great reward, which was promised at the completion of the sorting and classifying of their significant collection.

What first aroused my suspicion, was that the letters, while appearing to be in different handwriting, all shared certain similarities in their handwriting style, as if they had, in reality, been written by the same person. I only needed to determine who had actually written them. I confirmed that this was true, when my associate, Dr. Watson provided me with samples of your actual penmanship, as well as that of your caretaker, James. In addition, while each letter requested my presence, each one also asked, that I not mention that I had been requested to come. This also raised my suspicion, that what was being stated was not what it seemed. It was obvious that the author of the three letters did not want any of you to know that my presence had been requested by yourselves.

It appeared that someone was using the three of you to set up a scenario that was turning you all against each other. That someone was James, your caretaker. His plan was to create doubt and division between you, plant incriminating evidence to implicate each of you, and then have a third party come in and witness the final stroke. Once completed, this would remove all three of you from the property. If you recall, when my associate, Dr. Watson, was visiting, on the pretense of seeing the coprolite specimens, it came very close to two you of being arrested, Miss Beryl for perceived threats with a gun, which James had planted, Miss Amethyst, for stealing the specimens he had also planted, and the third, Miss Amber being committed for allegedly hearing the voices of her deceased parents giving her directions. James created that illusion by using a servant's speaking tube, that went from the guest room, which years ago, was a servant's room, to her room, which had been one of the main bedrooms. There he whispered to her, giving the impression that they were speaking to her. It was he that told her to look for the gun that he had planted. And of course, her delusional conversations were enough to concern Miss Amethyst.

You can thank Doctor Watson for calming things down. Had James succeeded that would have eliminated all three of you and left the classifying of the collection incomplete.

Why is that important, you may ask. Because then your great reward would have been forfeit. He was the caretaker not only of the estate, but of the reward. Being that he had worked for your parents for many years on their field expeditions, they felt they could trust him with one final task, overseeing the completion of their final request of you, to sort, classify, and catalog their massive collection. Once that was finished, he was to present the three of you with the great reward.

And what is this long-awaited reward? It is not exactly what you might have speculated. From what I have been told, you are quite near the completion of your monumental sorting task, so considering the current situation, I do not think your parents would mind you knowing in advance, what the reward is to be. When the task is finished the collection is to be placed in a special museum named after you three, The Beryl, Amber, and Amethyst Buckland Museum of Geology and Paleontology.

Your parents explained everything in a letter to you three, which was kept in a safe, in James's quarters, along with carved marble nameplates for each of your desks. A museum building had been purchased prior to their passing and was maintained by a trust fund. Once the task was completed, James was to present you the letter and nameplates and help in moving the collection to the museum that was to immortalize your names in history. That was their reward and final gift to you three.

However, William Buckland's eccentricity was very well known. Yes, even I have heard the stories of his strange appetite, which included panther, mouse, and even the preserved heart of a French king. So, it is not really surprising, that if you had not completed task and had abandoned it, then per his letter, Jame was authorized to auction the collection off, to other museums, and keep a twenty-five percent fee for his efforts. With the size of the collection being what it is, that would still be a considerable sum. The museum building would then have been sold as well. So, you see he had much to gain, by you three not completing your task. But, as long as the work continued, he was to continue helping and wait until its completion. Although it may seem harsh that your father would have even considered such an idea, he did leave notes of encouragement in the diaries of your parent's field expeditions. The rhymes that Miss Amber had been reciting, were clearly meant to give you hope and provide inspiration and incentive. He really wanted you three to complete the task.

Over the years James grew tired and produced a plan to remove the three of you, and end his wait, while increasing his financial gain. If he could have someone of my reputation verify the accusations against you three, accusations that he himself had perpetrated, then it would be done, and he would have his reward. However, he did not imagine that I would see right through his plan. The letters were an immediate clue, and when Doctor Watson reported to me what had occurred during his visit, I knew I had to act quickly. I paid a late-night visit to James, and confronted him with my theory, and the facts that he was already guilty of three counts of forgery, as well as the attempted framing of two of you. He has confessed, surrendered your parent's letter, and has been arrested, which is why he was not present this morning.

On a side note, to Miss Amethyst, I will confess, that your intended, Roger Rathmore, was also a possible suspect, and I examined his handwriting as well, in the note containing his address, that he gave to Dr. Watson. While his enthusiasm for your parent's collection may equal his admiration of you, he was not a part of the scheme.

The letter from your parents, along with your carved marble nameplates, is awaiting you three, on the desk in his quarters. I trust that knowing in advance what your great reward is, will not diminish your efforts to complete the task. I wish you the very best in your new status as museum founders and namesakes. After all, it is not just anyone who is immortalized in the name of a museum.

Sincerely,
Sherlock Holmes,
Consulting Detective

A Sherlockian Christmas

I'm dreaming of a Sherlockian Christmas,
just like those of long ago,
when the clues do glisten,
Holmes and Watson listen,
to hear footsteps in the snow.

I'm wondering, of where could they lead to?
Perhaps a winter's, Wisteria lodge?
Or a Red Circle, bright,
shinning in the night,
when bullets, they will have to dodge.

I'm pondering on Bruce Parington's Plans,
You know it keeps my thoughts afloat,
more than a Dying Detective.
It is really quite effective.
Just like, a secret submarine boat.

I'm musing on Lady Frances Carfax,
and also, of, The "You Know Who's" Foot.
And Sherlock's Last Bow
won't really be, we all know,
or Doyle would be quite hard put.

Yes, I'm dreaming of a Sherlockian Christmas
with every rhymed line I write.
May your clues be clear and so bright,
and may all your deductions be right.

Sherlock Holmes and Mrs. Hudson's Mystery

1st letter

Mrs. Hudson's Lodgings
221-b Baker Street
London, England
2, May, 1898

Dear Sherlock,

Please excuse me for having left this missive with your breakfast. Due to your extremely unpredictable schedule recently, I never know when you are here or gone. I only know that you have been here because the breakfast that I leave on your table every day is gone when I come to collect the dishes. At least I hope that it is you who is devouring it.

Honestly, you are a true master at entering and exiting your room without making any noise or being noticed, and I must say, you could give those magicians at the London theater a run for their money. That is not to say I want you to start performing decapitation illusions in your room. It is chaotic and untidy enough as it is. However, none of the above pertains to the reason for this letter.

I am writing to you because a dear friend of mine, Esmeralda Emerson, finds herself in a situation which has left her fully stymied. She is at a loss as to what to do, and if you could find the time to help her, I would be eternally grateful. I might even excuse the most recent bullet holes I noticed in the wall of your flat.

Esmeralda's situation is rather unusual. Like myself, she also rents out a set of upstairs rooms. While daily life with her current lodger has been, up until recently, uneventful, recent events have led to conflict with her tenant. She tells me her lodger is someone who holds a lofty position as an engineer for the government. She is not at large to say who he is, but he sounds quite important. Apparently, he has stated on more than one occasion that his work is more critical than she could ever imagine. The man is, to no surprise, very particular about his living arrangements, and has even provided a detailed schedule of exactly when Esmeralda may enter his room for cleaning. He has specified how long she may remain, (only 15 minutes during his 8:00 morning constitutional, which he takes after he has finished his 7:30 am breakfast) and what may or may not be cleaned. His desk, and anything on it are never to never touched. Yet of course he demands the premises be kept spotless.

The problem at hand is that yesterday he stormed into Esmeralda's own apartment claiming that while he was away at lunch, someone had gotten into a locked drawer where he keeps his work papers. Everything was still there, but not in the exact order he left it, and the drawer had been left unlocked. He said that it was simply inconceivable that he would have left the room with the drawer unlocked, and even worse, two sheets of paper were 'not in the right sequence.' He demanded an explanation, insisting he was positive about the way he had left it, and saying that his work simply can not be compromised. If it were, their very lives would be in danger. Nowhere would it be safe. Esmeralda said that she explained that no one had been to the house that day. She also illustrated   to him that people often make simple memory mistakes by asking him to close his eyes and name what color tie he was wearing that day.

The man was astonished when he could not recall the color without looking, but he insisted that his attire, and the nature of his work, were two entirely different subjects.

Obviously, papers in a locked drawer do not change position on their own. The uncertainty in this situation is not something one can just take to the local constables. They want hard facts, and bodies on the floor, not just papers out of order. That is why I am contacting you.

Esmeralda contacted me because I have mentioned you are my lodger. She is well aware of your reputation for solving perplexing mysteries based on the smallest of clues, and was hoping you might help. The implications of important government work being compromised are a critical concern. Is it possible that someone has gotten into his work papers? Even if nothing has been taken, Esmerelda worries that an intruder may have accessed her lodger's quarters. Whether or not the man's work papers are truly as important as he claims they are, my friend faces the possibility of losing a tenant should anything more serious occur, and if secret government work were to be stolen, it is possible that she might be held responsible.

Knowing your attention to the smallest detail, I asked her to recount anything unusual or otherwise 'different' that might have happened in the days leading up to the incident.

While she is positive that no one entered the house that day, she did mention several possible items of interest. Two days before the incident, right about dusk, she experienced a problem with a rattling noise. Something from above was making a noticeable amount of noise, and her lodger was growing irritated. Esmeralda says it is as if small creatures were scurrying about in the attic above the lodger's room. Yet prior to that day, she had never had any problems of that nature. Just after the disturbance, she stepped out of her door to see what she could on the exterior of the roof, only to notice right outside, a blond fellow holding a cage and a large briefcase. Esmeralda recalls that the cage only seemed small because of the man's rather muscular arms. She thanked her lucky stars when the tradesman introduced himself as a pest removal specialist, 'A-1 Rodent Removal Service', who was advertising his services to our vicinity. She hired him on the spot. He went up into the attic with his briefcase, cage, and a coil of rope, spent a short time there, and to her surprise, emerged with several dead rats in the cage. The gentleman, a Mr. Bauer, said that if she had any additional problems, he would come back and take care of the situation at no additional cost. She noted that he had a rather thick German accent.

Apart from this, Mrs. Emerson received two different offers for free cleaning services. The day after the rattling noise, a tradesman representing 'William's Wondrous Window Washing' came to her door, offering to clean the exterior windows of her building free of charge. The offer was meant to demonstrate his new cleaning method and products. Esmeralda admits that this seemed like a wonderful idea to her, and she agreed. He said he would be there the following day as early as he could be. Esmeralda seems to think he did a wonderful job and confirms that he never entered the building to her knowledge. All their windows are locked from the inside, except for the upper windows.

The second offer came from a gentleman promoting his newly invented suction powered cleaning device. He offered Esmeralda a free floor cleaning service, saying that it was a special opportunity to raise awareness of his unique cleaning method. It involves a device similar to the powered carpet sweeper invented by the American, Daniel Hess, but it is somewhat bigger. The contraption involves a large box with hoses attached to it. The box contains an apparatus that powers the cleaning device, which collects dirt and dust before transferring it into a 'containment section'. I was truthfully impressed by Esmeralda's ability to explain the machine. It all sounds rather complicated if you ask me, but she says the vendor believes it will soon be a feature of every home. Of course, by that time, he claims the machine will be available in a much smaller size, but he needs to make people aware of it before any of that can happen.

The gentleman said the device would need to remain in her building for a full three days in order to effectively demonstrate its capabilities. This offer also sounded truly intriguing, so Esmeralda agreed. He had the device brought in and placed in the hallway and said he would be back the next day to begin the cleaning service.

I do understand that you are extremely busy at the moment, but as I explained, her lodger's work is particularly important, and she is quite concerned.

Sincerely,
Mrs. Hudson

2nd letter

May 5, 1898
Nigel Nextworth M.E.
London, England
3, May, 1898

Dear Mr. Holmes,

I have been referred to you by a gentleman with whom I am acquainted with in my government work. His name is Mycroft. I did not get his last name, but perhaps you know of him. I am certain that somebody has been tampering with my important work documents, which are normally kept in a securely locked drawer. I am requesting your aid in resolving this situation with the utmost discretion.

You will have to excuse my vagueness: I am an engineer working for the crown. I am not at liberty to divulge any details concerning my current project, but my calculations are extremely critical to our military, and our country's security, as well as the very safety of our citizens. Due to concerns regarding the considerable number of employees at my particular office, I have followed the suggestion of a government observer, to work from home in my apartment. My rooms are on the second floor, where it is quiet, secure, and most of all, very private.

I first realized something was amiss when I returned from lunch yesterday. I found my desk drawer unlocked, which I would never do, and upon removing my work, I noticed that two sheets were not in the exact order I had left them. Nothing else was disturbed, and nothing was actually missing,

I at once went to see my landlady, Mrs. Esmeralda Emerson, and she assured me that no one besides herself had been in the building while I was away. She suggested that perhaps because I was in a hurry, I had simply failed to lock the drawer, and place them in the order I had thought. She even offered a trite example of people's forgetfulness. Mr. Holmes, I am most meticulous in my habits. I have created checklists for every aspect of my daily schedule and even have checklists to verify my checklists. I am certain of how I left things. That is why I am contacting you. The evidence I offer, may seem small, but I assure you, the implications are profound. The question must be answered, could there be another explanation? Considering her shallow reassurances, could she be the intruder?

My schedule is like clockwork. The only times during the day, that I am away from my work area are when I go out for a thirty-minute lunch in the early afternoon, at exactly 12:30 pm, and again at 6:00 pm, when I take my evening meal, which lasts precisely forty-five minutes. Of course, I always keep all my work papers securely locked in my desk drawer on these occasions. I also lock the door to my workspace, as well as the door to the entire flat. The room in which I work does not have a window, so I am confident that no one could gain access from the exterior. There are windows in my parlour, but they are always kept locked.

Up until recently, the flat has been a place where I can easily concentrate without fear of interruption. Mrs. Emerson has always been most accommodating and respectful of my privacy. I have provided her a detailed schedule of when and how my work and personal spaces are to be cleaned, and she has complied quite well. Until now, I have had full confidence in her honesty and would not have believed that she could have any part in the issue at hand.

I will relate to you the only unusual things that I have witnessed in the days leading up to the incident. Firstly, several days ago, near nightfall, I noticed a noise in the attic space above my work area, like some small animal was rustling around. I mentioned this to Mrs. Emerson, and she surprisingly found someone to help within minutes. The tradesman was quickly able to collect and remove several rats that had somehow found their way up to the attic. The rattling sound was eliminated, but I still hear an occasional creaking sound. I have inspected the attic myself since then but have found nothing out of the ordinary.

The attic features a wooden planked floor, and wooden beams running transversely across the width of the building. Mrs. Emerson keeps the building fairly tidy, but scraps of newspaper and tiny amounts of dirt and crumbs litter the attic floor. It hosts several boxes, trunks, wicker cases, and forgotten decorations. The usual items that one might expect. A large window overlooking the back of the property is at the far back of the space, nearly framed by two of the wooden ceiling beams. Just against the beam nearest to the window sits a dusty case of, mostly, gardening equipment. Shears, several spades, several mismatched gloves, some rope, and a small trowel. I did notice rope fibers on top of the ceiling beam that is situated in directly front of the back window. This window is kept locked from the inside as well.

Otherwise, Mrs. Emerson recently had two separate cleaning services tend to the property. First, she mentioned that the building's exterior windows would be washed, but that it would not affect the interior of the building. Before I went to lunch that day, I verified that all my windows were securely latched, and when I returned, they were just as I had left them.

In the days after this, Mrs. Emerson received an offer to have her carpets cleaned at no cost. The gentleman, a Mr. Hubert Booth, was hoping to promote his new contraption, an oversized machine that relies on a 'suction tube'. After Mrs. Emerson accepted his offer, he left a large box, containing the mechanical suction device, in the hallway of the building. Mr. Booth claimed he was an engineer as well, one who has designed bridges as well as ferris wheels. I have looked over his device. There are several dials on the side, a cable that plugs into the electricity available in the building, and a hose attachment with a narrow opening on its end. I presume that is the 'business end', which draws in the dirt. The gentleman instructed Mrs. Emerson to leave the machine be for two days, the duration of its 'cleaning period'. He assured her that his vacuum powered cleaning devices would soon be all the rage, but I honestly cannot see that happening. The device is unspeakably cumbersome. I see no future in it unless it is drastically reduced in size. Its overly large dimensions have also been a personal concern. The large box holding the apparatus that powers the machine especially troubles me.

You are, of course, familiar with 'The Turk', the famous chess playing machine, built in 1770 by Wolfgang von Kempelen. Presented as a clockwork automaton, it was a mechanical device that played an extraordinarily strong game of chess. Kempelen would typically open various doors in the device to show that there was just machinery inside, but in truth, its function was to conceal a master chess player hidden within. It deceived everyone who examined it for over eighty years. After all, when he opened the doors, one could see nothing but the gears and cogs. How could it be hiding anything? While my field of expertise is engineering, and I have perused the machine, I can only think back to the countless "experts" who were utterly fooled by the The Turk. I did inspect the apparatus to the best of my abilities and cannot imagine a person existing within, though the thought still crosses my mind on occasion.

From what Mr. Mycroft, has said about you, nothing escapes your exceptional observation and deduction skills, and you could resolve this situation. Do let me know if this would be possible, and I will advise my landlady accordingly.

Sincerely,
Nigel Nextworth

3rd letter

Mycroft Holmes
The Diogenes Club
London, England

3 May, 1898

Greetings Brother,

If you have not yet received a query from a Mr. Nigel
Nextworth, Mechanical Engineer, I imagine you will quite
soon. Mr. Nextworth is working on an important project for
the crown, and due to the number of persons who have
access to the project office, it was decided (by myself) that
for the current phase of his work, (very critical calculations,
easily done on paper, in the privacy of his lodgings,) that he
should work from his home. As you would deduce, his
lodgings and his landlady have been thoroughly verified as
secure. In fact, I believe that his landlady is a friend of your
Mrs. Hudson.

Things had been going quite well, but I have recently been
informed of a possible breach in security. He is certain that
someone may have accessed his locked work papers
drawer, while he was away at lunch. He brought it up to his
landlady, who attempted to dismiss his concern, but there
does remain some degree of uncertainty, both in her
reasoning, as well as his claim. However, as this particular
project offers a breakthrough for the military, there is no
room, whatsoever, for doubt. He is working on calculations
for the military; cutting edge, technological developments,
which if they got into the wrong hands, some of our fiercest
competitors would gain access to elite military strategies,
and some of our most advanced weaponry. Sherlock, I can

not strongly enough stress the importance of this situation. We must have an indisputable answer. That is where you enter the picture.

There are three possible leads. One involves a pest exterminator who happened to appear, two days prior to the incident, precisely as the need arose. The other two, were offers of free cleaning services. One occurred the day of the purported break-in, while the other, a floor cleaning demonstration, is still in progress. I hear from my sources that a number of different service providers have recently been offering free demonstrations to increase their business in the city, but the timing of these offers at this particular location does make them rather suspect.

Returning to the pest exterminator, he managed to trap some rats that had found themselves into the attic, and left without any issues. I have inquired into the first cleaner, and he seems to be legitimate, as he has made this same offer to several other building owners in the city. He cleans one set of windows in a neighborhood, does an exceptional job, and then charges a higher-than-normal fee to all the referrals, making up the cost of the free cleaning. It is rather clever actually.

The floor cleaning gentleman, I believe requires more investigation. His device involves a large box which provides the motive operation that powers the system and collects the dirt. It is to remain on the premises the entire time of his 'demonstration'. Due to its size, (the box is three feet wide, by four feet long, by four feet high). Do not ask how I know this. It is my duty to know anything that is of vital importance to the crown. (Except, of course, the solution to problems that are not easily resolved which is why I am writing to you.) the box could easily conceal someone who would then have access to the room while he was away. I am certain that if you could pay a visit to his lodgings, you could resolve the entire situation. Nothing escapes your calibrated eye. Yes, I know that my vision is equal to yours, and I would pay a visit to his lodging, except I do not leave the building unless it an absolute emergency, for example, the building is on fire.

Mr. Nextworth, in spite of being an excellent engineer, and meticulous to a fault, is quite timid in nature, and although he has inspected the machine, I am sure he would not have done it as rigorously as yourself. However, he has added an extra lock to the drawer, and a padlock on the door to his office.

Despite these new precautions, there is new evidence, in the form of very subtle dusty footprints in the hallway, that someone other than the Mrs. Emerson, the landlady, Mr. Nextworth, and the cleaner, has passed through the hall. Besides the three of them, no one else has any business inside that building.

Even more concerning, is that two blank sheets of paper, unlike the type of paper he uses, were found under his desk, when he returned from lunch just recently. Being as fastidious as he is, especially in light of the current situation, it is unlikely that Mr. Nextworth would have left any papers on the floor, even more so, since they are not even the brand of paper he uses. That brings up the question, how did they get there, and by whom were they left? Once again, his landlady claims no knowledge of how they may have gotten there, but here is the really significant factor. The blank sheets are the same type of stationary that Mrs. Emerson has on her desk, just inside her flat. Could she be the culprit?

As always, my involvement in your efforts regarding this matter must remain unspoken. Do keep me informed and try not delay too long.

Your brother,
Mycroft

4th letter

Mrs. Hudson's Lodgings
221-b Baker Street
London, England
May 4, 1898

Dear Sherlock,

I found your brief reply in the remnants of your breakfast today. Thank you. I am so glad you are looking into this. Now strange things have started occurring in Esmerelda's flat as well as her lodgers's. Just yesterday, when he returned early from lunch, he found errant stationary on the floor beneath his desk, and that he felt he was being watched, even though there was no one else in the room. He said he could not shake the feeling of an additional presence, and he came down to Esmeralda's flat to ask if someone had been there while he was away. While he was in her parlour, he recognized the sheets he found, as being the same as those on her desk. She could not explain it as she had been out at the market while he was at lunch. She did notice her desk had also been disturbed and mentioned it to him, but he was quite skeptical. When he returned to his flat, he noticed that the heavy widow curtain in the parlour area had been significantly disturbed, but the sense of someone else being there had decreased.

Even today, although his work papers were not out of numerical order, and the drawer was still locked when he returned from lunch, his papers did not look "right" to him. He was certain that they had been handled again, as they were not physically situated in the drawer exactly as he had left them. He also said that the locks were not positioned exactly as he had left them. Really, how many ways can a padlock be positioned in a hasp? Did I mention, he added a second lock to the drawer? He is genuinely concerned that his work is being comprised and has threatened to terminate his lease if the situation is not resolved immediately!

In your reply, you asked about the cleaning device, the box is sitting in the entry hallway of her lodgers flat, along with the various tubes that are used for the actual cleaning. From what I have been told, the gentleman providing the device did a very quick demonstration for her in the hallway and produced a considerable amount of debris in the collection box. She was flabbergasted and rather mortified at the amount of material it collected. She has always prided herself in the cleanliness of her lodgings.

Again, per your request, she was able to measure the box and obtain the dimensions you asked for. They were, if I recall correctly, three feet wide, by four feet long, by four feet high. One of your little street ruffians, I believe you refer to them as Baker Street Irregulars, was right outside her door when she finished measuring, and I have been told, was able to bring them to you, much quicker than I would have thought possible.

However, speaking of small, one odd bit of information, that I would like to share, is that sometime after the initial cleaning demonstration was completed, Esmeralda had to step out to go to the market, while her lodger was also away at lunch. (Of course, the premises were securely locked.) When she returned and again passed through the hallway, she noticed crumbs on the floor. They started near the door to Mr. Nextworth's flat, going past the doorway up to the attic, which is on the way out. Or is it the opposite? Either way, she is certain, the crumbs were not there when the demonstration was completed. Esmeralda says she paused by the device for several minutes to listen, but did not hear anything at all inside. Is it possible that her lodger was simply nibbling on a biscuit while he worked, leaving a mess of crumbs on his way out?

Esmeralda also says that since the pest exterminator was there, she has noticed some general creaking of the upper portion of her building. She claims it has become rather awful lately, but she attributes that to the age of the structure and the wind outside. Mr. Nextworth told Esmeralda that he had already investigated the attic, but just to be certain, she did go up and have a quick peek. She noticed the same crumbs on the floor up there as well. They were near some of the large wicker trunks, and around her old gardening equipment. I would say Mr. Nextworth should be more mindful of where he eats his food.

In any case, as per your reply, I am pleased that you have been investigating and feel confident in your observations so far. I am not certain what exactly you meant by "Things are looking up.", but it is good to know that all will be resolved soon. Both Esmeralda and myself appreciate your help.

Your Humble Landlady,
Mrs. Hudson

5rh letter

Sherlock Holmes
221-b Baker Street
London, England
5, May, 1898

Dear Mycroft,

Having already written to Mr. Nextworth, and to my
landlady, Mrs. Hudson, who has shared her letter with his
landlady, Mrs. Emerson, I finally am writing to you. I am
writing, but I am also certain, that with your omnipresent
awareness and connections, you already know my
conclusion and the end result, but you did ask me to keep
you informed.

You were correct in saying that Mrs. Emerson is not a
security risk. Through Mrs. Hudson, she sought my help as
soon as the issue materialized. Even though she had offered
a plausible explanation for his concern, Mrs. Emerson, and
Mr. Nextworth were both right to be concerned about his
work papers being compromised. While either of the two
offers of free cleaning services could have been a possible
problem, they ultimately served more as red herrings to
distract from the real danger, the pest removal service, A-1
Rodent Removal Service, which was a front for a Mr. Karl
Bauer, a German agent, whom I am aware of. Up until now,
he has eluded capture, but he has been involved in other
espionage cases involving military secrets. Both Mrs.
Emerson, and Mr. Nextworth, mentioned the noises
upstairs, and the removal of several dead rats, but did not
give it any credit, and even you did not seem overly
concerned. But he was the access point for his accomplice
to gain entry into the flat.

If you recall, the event occurred at dusk, when the lighting was very low. In the shadows, unseen, the pest remover's accomplice was throwing pebbles and small stones up to the roof and letting them roll down. This created the scurrying noise that Mr. Nextworth noticed. Of course, the pest remover was already waiting near the front entrance, ready to be of service. The briefcase he carried with him, held the already dead rats which he claimed to trap on the property, as well as a long rope, which he lowered to his accomplice from the attic window. He then left the rope behind in the attic, where it would remain unnoticed by Mrs. Emerson's gardening tools. The accomplice remained hidden in a wicker trunk. With a small food supply. (the source of the crumbs) Inside his hiding place, he could observe and listen for when it was safe to come out, typically, when Mr. Nextworth left for lunch and dinner. Mr. Nextworth was very precise in the timing of his meal arrangements. When the premises were empty, being an accomplished picklock, the spy was able to gain access to Mr. Nextworth's workspace and desk. He would make copies of the calculations and return the originals to their original location in the drawer, so nothing was out of order, and he could continue gathering information unnoticed. His error was leaving the sheets out of sequence, which raised Mr. Nextworth's suspicions. Forgetting to re-lock the drawer when he was done, was also a obvious clue. On top of that there were the subtle footprints that you reported. Any time someone walks through a dusty area such as an attic, their shoes will gather dust which will then be left behind on a freshly cleaned surface such as the hallway. (I have written a monograph on dusty footprints which clearly points out the process. I think you would enjoy reading it.)

In addition, the spy was almost revealed the day Mr. Nextworth did not follow his usual routine and returned from lunch early. You will recall that he strongly felt a presence and went down to the landlady's flat to talk to her and ask about the sheets found on the floor. When he returned, the curtain in the adjoining room had been disturbed. The accomplice had heard Nigel returning, panicking, he left the two sheets on the floor, and quickly hid in the only place available, behind the window curtain in the parlour. It was a heavy enough curtain that Mr. Nextworth did not see the intruder. When he he returned from talking to his landlady, the spy had returned to his hiding place in the attic.

The spy had been getting more careless everyday, even to the point of "borrowing" stationary from Mrs. Emerson's desk and leaving crumbs as he went back and forth from his attic hiding place.

Fortunately, the spy could only collect the information and keep it in his hiding space until his accomplice came back to retrieve him, so none of the copies ever left the attic. In addition, the spy was just copying highly technical information which made no sense to him, similar to someone making a copy of a page written in a foreign language that they did not understand. The calculations have not been comprised, and the project is safe. From what I understand, if they had been successful, even London itself would have been in great danger.

The plan was, to later in the week, make more scurrying noises upstairs, which would require the return of the pest remover, at no additional cost, to address the situation, and while he was there, let the spy back down the rope, lock the window, and leave with the rope and copied calculations in his briefcase. It was a clever scheme actually, but the rope fibers on the ceiling beam near the attic window, the creaking upstairs, the dusty footprints, the crumbs on the floor in the hallway after the cleaning demonstration, and upstairs in the attic, the errant pages of copying paper, and Mrs. Emerson's desk being disturbed, were all telltale clues that the culprit was in the premises the whole time.

As, I am sure Mr. Nextworth informed you, I paid a visit to him just prior to his going out to dinner yesterday, and I explained my theory. I quietly informed him that he was to lock me in his work area, and then loudly pretend to be talking to me as he left for dinner. The spy then thought we had left together and again came out of hiding to access Mr. Nextworth's work area. He was not expecting me to be waiting for him inside. Apprehending him was quite straightforward, and he provided the information which facilitated the capture of his accomplice, Mr. Bauer, the pest removal specialist.

Mr. Nextworth's calculations are safe, and the premises are actually, quite clean, but I would not invest in the powered cleaning invention at this time. It is simply too large and cumbersome. I would suggest waiting until it can be reduced in size and perhaps be made more mobile. I am certain that with his credentials in bridge design, as well as ferris wheels, Mr. Booth will someday achieve success with it. I understand, he was offered a knighthood but turned it down.

While I must say that you were wise to inform me of this situation, the landlady, Mrs. Emerson, was also most observant, and quick to request my help. Thanks to her, and Mrs. Hudson's inspired comments on magician's abilities to enter and leave spaces unnoticeable, I was already formulating my thoughts on this case when I received yours and Mr. Nextworth's letters. She is to be commended.

Sincerely,
Sherlock

The Untold tales of Sherlock Holmes

There are stories of Sherlock Holmes untold,
their clues mysterious, ancient and old.
For reasons, one may never share,
the secrets, Watson will not dare

reveal more than just a word,
a hint, a whisper, how absurd!
Yet, if you look within the story,
they are there in all their glory.

The time that Holmes was summoned to
Odessa for a murder new,
Trepoff was the name they say
untold even to this day.

And the singular tragedy,
of the Atkinson brothers at Trincomalee.
If known, the bards would surely sing
of the remarkably brilliant ring

that Holmes received for his success.
What he did, who can guess?
Twas' a delicate case you see,
for Holland's reigning family.

The Darlignton substitution scandal,
Holmes did magnificently handle.
The Arnsworth castle fire trick
provided answers very quick.

(He's used this ruse more than one time
to solve a mystery or a crime.)
And if a secret no one knows
can be famous, the one I chose

is the ship Matilda Briggs,
(not for her mast, or sails, or rigs)
but for a giant Sumatran rat.
Can you even imagine that?

Yet, the world can never know,
so untold this case will go.
But there are those who digging deep
into imagination steep,

have uncovered cases strange
and before your eyes arrange
stories lost to ages past
that grab your imagination fast.

They'll astound, and feast your senses
when the reading, it commences.
Yes, they sure will rattle your bones
The untold cases of Sherlock Holmes.

Sherlock Holmes and The Wonderland Garden

1st letter

From the Desk of
Reginald Rodricks III

23 June, 1898

Dear Mr. Holmes,

My name is Reginald Rodricks III, and you are my last
hope. I am turning to you to solve the mystery of what has
become of my late father's fortune. It is gone, and the thief
has somehow managed to do so seemingly under our very
own eyes! All of the money that was in his bank accounts,
as well as the considerable proceeds from the recent sale
of his business have mysteriously vanished, and I am at a
loss as to where to turn.

You may have read in the papers that my father, Reginald
Rodricks II, recently passed away; actually, he was lost at
sea in a sailing accident, on June sixteenth, of this year. An
extensive search of the coastal area where he went
overboard was conducted, but his body was never
recovered. It was after a week of searching, that his long-
time advisor and solicitor, Edwin Grabington, approached
my brother and I with the will, and pointed out that it clearly
stated that it was to come into effect at his death, or his
disappearance, waiting no more than exactly one week. (As
eccentric as he was, he was always very precise and
punctual about things.) We had a private, (just my brother
and I and our family butler) memorial ceremony, which is
what he had requested in his will. The will divided the
house and garden between us, with me getting the house,

and Robert getting the adjacent Wonderland Garden, (I will mention more about that later.), but there was no mention of our father's actual physical funds. It was like the money did not exist. It must have gone somewhere. We examined his bank accounts and the safe that he kept in his office at home and there was nothing! The accounts and safe were empty. My brother, Robert, and I were dumbfounded.

The will started out apologetically. He said that he felt he had failed us, and that he was sorry that my brother and I could not have gotten along better. (Robert and I are always at odds, over almost everything, especially the way father handled his finances. I felt he should only invest in his metal casting business, to expand and increase it, while Robert only encouraged him to read fictional adventures and go off on wild goose chase expeditions.) He went on to say that it would have been his greatest wish for us to get along, and be real brothers, that he did make many attempts over the years to convince us to get along, and that he can not rest in peace without knowing that we have reconciled. He even said, that compared to true friendship between brothers, money was nothing, and that without it we would finally learn to work together. That may be, Mr. Holmes, but money is necessary to get on in life, and I assure you, my father had amassed a considerable amount of money over the course of his lifetime. He was a daring and bold businessman, and thought nothing of taking great risks, which almost always paid off for him. He also earned a considerable sum from the sale of his business. And now it is all gone! The will made no mention of any cash assets at all. It was as if they had just vanished! I assure you; something is very foul here. I believe someone has bilked him out of his fortune, and we must discover who it was.

As I previously mentioned, I get the house and Robert gets the garden. Father's motor yacht was left to the family butler. (This is not surprising, since he has served our father for so long, and did all the care and maintenance on the motor yacht.) while his sailing yacht, "Checkmate" is to remain in permanent joint ownership between my brother and I. (When the three of us went sailing together, those were the few times my brother and I came close to getting along, so maybe he is hoping that it will bring us together. I do not see much chance of that happening.) Mr. Grabington has offered to purchase the yacht from us should we decide to sell it. He said that he could easily handle all the details regarding permanent ownership and would be happy to take it off our hands.

The will ends by saying that, if we have any concern for his earthly peace of mind, or his eternal peace, my brother and I should have a "Heart to Heart" conversation with the Queen of Hearts in the garden, at the entrance to her castle, and be sure to bring the gold heart pendants that were given to the two of us on our 21st birthday. I honestly have no idea what that is about. He gave the heart pendants he mentioned to both of us when we turned 21, and said while we may not want to wear them, never, ever lose them. I have not given any thought to them until the reading of the will. As I previously stated, he was really, quite eccentric, and his request seems rather meaningless, compared to the real issue of the missing funds.

Our family has always been moderately well to do, and by family, I mean my late father, my twin brother and myself. Our mother died many years ago when we were very young, and he never remarried. He poured himself into his business, and if I may say so, any number of strange, eccentric endeavours. It has always been just the three of us, and our family butler of course. Father felt that he had no need for added staff, as William took care of all domestic and driver duties. He did spend considerable time with his solicitor, as in addition to professional business, they enjoyed solving riddles and puzzles together. They particularly liked the logic puzzles of Lewis Carroll. From what I understand they were fiercely competitive and would regularly bet on the outcome of the riddles, and who could solve them quicker. They had quite a rivalry going in that aspect, and although he never shared specific details it seemed that the bets between them grew more outlandish over time.

My brother and I, although we are twins, (I am the eldest.), we were always at odds for our father's attention while we were growing up. We never saw eye to eye on anything. I chose to take an interest in my father's metal-casting business early on, and I had worked my way up, becoming second in charge, until he just recently sold it. My brother on the other hand, was an unconventional free spirit, and had chosen a literary career, becoming a librarian, of all things. The frustrating aspect of it all is that my father, in his eccentricity, grew much closer to him than to I, who had put in so much effort into his business. Robert, my brother, would suggest a book to my father, who after reading it would become so obsessed with it that he would dive into any matter of hare-brained ideas involving that story. For example, after reading Jules Verne's "A Journey to the Centre of the Earth," he and my brother left for a several month trip to Iceland, to visit Snæfellsjökull, the mountain which led to the centre of the Earth in the novel. He hired a guide service, "Hans will get you there, Guide Service", at considerable expense, I might add, to lead them through the mountains of Iceland. While he was off gallivanting, trying to find a fictional entrance to the interior of the Earth,

115

I was running the family business. They also spent several months sailing the Caribbean, again with the same guide service from their Iceland expedition, after reading "Treasure Island." How ludicrous is that?

After reading H. G. Wells' "The Time Machine" He hired an inventor/scientist, fellow, a Dr. Alex Hardegan to work with him on the possibility of making a time machine of all things. After little progress was made, he dismissed him to start work on his next project, even though Dr. Hardegan claimed he was very close to a solution and only needed additional funding. He was rather upset when he was dismissed. I personally think he was a quack pot, taking advantage of my father, but there was no changing father's mind once he set his mind to something, no matter how strange, far fetched, or risky it was. Dr. Hardegan came by several times just before father disappeared to try and convince him to invest more funds in the project. He was most insistent that he could produce a solution, if only father invested more funds. He had even gotten added support from other sources but still needed more.

My father's most recent, (just before he passed away) and if I might add, most eccentric behaviour, occurred just after reading "Alice's Adventures in Wonderland" and "Through the Looking Glass." He came up with the idea to purchase the property directly next to our home and have a "Wonderland Garden" constructed there. In addition to the usual trees, plants, flowers and pathways, there is a large garden-size chess board, with over-sized chess pieces; (the King is two feet tall, and the pawns are one foot tall.) a croquet court with flamingo shaped mallets, croquet balls painted to look like hedgehogs, hoops made to look like the playing card guards; numerous life-sized, fully painted, statues of Alice and the other characters; and to top it off, a building made to look like a smaller version of the Queen of Hearts' castle, with a statue of the Queen of Hearts standing right at the entrance! She is positioned to the right of the entrance door with her hand out as if asking for payment to enter the castle. The building itself houses an ornate, inlaid table with a chess board. and hefty metal chess pieces. It is quite impressive, even if it is a waste of money.

The garden property is nearly the same size as the grounds of the family house. It is gated, and fully fenced on the three sides that do not adjoin the main house. There are red and white rose hedges between the two properties, meandering pathways throughout the garden, and the Queen of Hearts castle sits directly in the centre of it all. Mr. Grabington worked closely with him in most of the purchases for construction of the garden, but many he handled entirely on his own. I do recall overhearing several heated discussions between them during that time, something about one final bet to end all bets, and father shouting in a loud voice, "You can bet on it!" Father never did explain what that was about. I honestly feel the entire endeavour was a colossal waste of money. He had even shut down paying production work in his metal casting business for a week to make his garden statues. Father was very skilled in all the aspects of metal casting, and liked to keep his hands in the process, which I understand, but it makes no sense to me to have stopped all work just to make all those ridiculous garden statues.

Returning to the missing funds, when he sold his business two weeks before his disappearance, he was paid in full. And per his special request, was paid in cash, gold crowns, to be specific, which amounted to a considerable amount of coinage. The expenses for all of his inane literary trips and the new Wonderland Garden are properly entered in the ledgers, and although I am no accountant, they seem to be legitimate. His solicitor assured me of that, but could Mr. Grabington have tampered with the ledgers? He did have access to all of father's financial matters. In addition, all of his bank withdrawals, which were also for gold crowns, over the last several months prior to his passing, are properly signed, but the house has been thoroughly searched by my brother and I, and there is no sign anywhere of the money that he withdrew, or the funds from the sale of his business. That is a considerable amount of gold. It can not have just vanished. Someone must must have absconded with the entire fortune. Mr Grabington has no answer as to what could have happened to the funds, as he did not monitor all fathers' activities. We questioned William, and he also said that being just a butler, and driver, he would have no idea what could have happened.

With the family business sold, I am no longer working, and with his bank account empty, I am at a loss where to turn. That money must be somewhere, but where? I am at a complete loss.

Which leads me to the rather strange matter of his passing. He took his sailing yacht out for a day sail, as he often did. He was an experienced sailor, and the vessel was rigged for single-handed sailing. When we were younger, we went sailing with the three of us, and those were some of the few times my brother and I almost got along, as we were all working towards a common goal. My father had always said, "It takes teamwork to get the most out of a sailing craft, and life is very much like a sailboat. Sometimes you must tack in a direction other than the way you want to go, but working together will get you there."

But, returning to the present, He left the harbour alone, on June sixteenth, and did not return at the expected time. With sailing, however, that can be explained, as the wind and currents can cause delays. But after some time went by, William, our family butler, became concerned and took the family motor yacht to head out and look for him. He found his boat abandoned not far from shore several miles down the coast from the harbour. There was no sign of violence or a struggle. The main halyard had parted, causing a loss of the mainsail, and based on the tools and items on the deck, it appeared that he had been trying to jury rig a repair to it, and somehow fell overboard. William towed the vessel back to port and we rented additional motor craft and started a search up and down the coast in that area, and when no trace was found, we expanded the search efforts for a full week, but with no success.

My brother and I were devastated. At first, we both pointed fingers at each other. I felt that since Robert was always going on those ridiculous trips with him, he should have been there to support our ageing father. Robert felt that since the business was gone, and I no longer had to keep things running efficiently, that I should have been there. We are barely speaking to each other at this point.

I am at my wits end, Mr. Holmes. Could it be Mr. Grabington who had access to his assets, or perhaps, could Robert have hidden the gold somewhere in the Wonderland Garden, since that project was his idea, and it was left to him? I assure you that I have inspected the garden to the best of my abilities. I have even scraped the surfaces of some of the statues to see if they are actually gold instead of bronze, but they do not appear to be. Your reputation for seeing the unseen precedes you Mr. Holmes. I am certain

119

that you will be able to discern what has happened to the gold and solve this mystery.

Sincerely,
Reginald Rodricks III

2nd letter

From the desk of
Robert Rodricks, MLS, LBR.

24 June, 1898

Dear Mr. Holmes,

By now you have already received a letter from my brother, Reginald, about our late father's estate, and his missing fortune, and I am certain it was rather one-sided in its description of events leading to our father's disappearance and presumed death. I feel compelled to relate to you the other side of the story. The only thing my brother and I agree on is the urgency in the matter of resolving what happened to his fortune.

He has told me, straight to my face, that he feels the missing funds could be cleverly hidden somewhere in the Wonderland Garden. I do not see how that would be possible, being that it is outdoors and in plain view at all times. It is true, I was quite involved in the construction of the garden and all the structures and statues, which is precisely how I know that there is no feasible way that a fortune could be hidden there. I personally feel that unless it was somehow secretly removed from the house by persons, yet unknown, the money may still be hidden somewhere in the family house. Yes, it has been searched, but an old sprawling home such as ours, could easily have hidden chambers. I did ask father's solicitor, who has handled all his finances to locate a set of blueprints for the house, but he said none were available. I even hired a well-respected builder to come out and examine the building and he did not find anything unusual.

Our cook/butler/driver, William, has said that he had not noticed anything unusual about our father's behaviour prior to the day he disappeared. He seemed happier than usual, but nothing more. The day that my father went out in his yacht, 'Checkmate', William took him to the harbour at 10 a.m., and was instructed to return at 4 p.m. He returned at the appointed time, but after waiting a short while, and not seeing any sign of the yacht approaching in the distance, he grew concerned and took out our family motor yacht. He went out to see if he could find him before nightfall. Luckily enough, William at once turned south, and in a short while, he found the yacht, abandoned, and drifting. As I am sure Reginald informed you, William towed it back to the harbour, and it has been kept there since the incident. The local constables examined the yacht thoroughly. They noted a parted main halyard, several tools to jury rig a repair on the cabin top, the main boom was not secured, and the jib sheets were loose, but everything else seemed in order. The fact that the main halyard had parted, strikes me as unusual, as father had just had his yacht hauled out for some maintenance and repairs. William assisted him with the much of the work, and since father's disappearance, he has been acting oddly, being very edgy, especially regarding the halyard, as if he feels responsible.

Regarding William, he has served our family for ages, in fact, since we were young lads, and I really do trust his word, or at least I thought I did. He has always been right there for our father, and he was almost like an uncle to my brother and me. He often shared sage advice, that we should try harder to get along together, how much that would really please our father, and that the day would come when we regret our petty foolishness. Being that he was the last person to see father alive, and he brought father's yacht back to port alone, could he be involved? It seems most unlikely, but here is one possible explanation. If the fortune is not located, he will be out of a job soon, as the severance money my brother received when the company was sold, will last only so long. Reginald may not be able to keep William employed, so he would have a strong motive, as much as it saddens me to say that. If he were released from his position, he could then leave the area with his fortune, and no one would be the wiser.

Of course, William primarily served father in his regular activities. With me being involved in my library work, and Reginald always being buried in the business affairs, William aided our father in his daily tasks, as well as regular household duties. He drove the hansom to father's various meetings and appointments. He was questioned after father's disappearance, and replied, "that his typical task as driver was to just transport father as needed and then wait outside with the carriage until he was finished. He did mention that just before the sale of the casting business was sold, during the evening after the shop was closed, he and a boat yard worker, Fredrick Granger, assisted father in moving many boxes of personal information and memorabilia from the casting business to our home, and then bringing more boxes back for additional loads.

Returning to the situation between my brother and I, my father's last request in the will, was that we have a heart-to-heart conversation at the Queen of Hearts castle, in the Wonderland Garden. We were requested to bring the heart pendants that we received for out 21st birthdays to the castle entrance, and that was all. In spite of everything going on, as strange as the request was, we finally decided it was the least we could do to honour our father. When we arrived for the conversation, we really did not know what to say, or for that matter, what to do. We were just begrudgingly fulfilling our father's last request. We remembered that he had said to bring the heart pendants so we both took them out, and were looking at them, wondering what to do, when I commented that the way the Queen of Hearts' hand was positioned, it appeared that she was demanding payment. Just out of curiosity, we placed the heart pendants in her hand, and it turned out they were not pure gold, but thinly plated magnets, which opened a panel that held an additional message from our father. You can imagine our shock and surprise! We both thought that this could be the answer to the missing funds, but we were wrong.

His message said that he was pleased that we had chosen to honour his request for the Queen of Hearts conversation and that we had found his additional note. There was nothing said about the missing funds, only another request. It merely stated, "If Robert and Reginald have truly overcome their petty rivalry and can show the cooperation and teamwork required to resolve one final question, and get to the bottom of the matter, their reward will be greater than either of them could imagine. The question is: 'With Knight to QB3 as the opening move, what is the optimum number of following moves that would please me?' Sit down at the chess table in the castle, play one final game for me, and answer the question."

I do understand that his question relates to a game of chess. Both my brother and I are experienced players and fiercely competitive. Our father taught us the game when we were quite young, and he was quite proud of both of our successes and achievements in chess. In fact, I recall that he and his solicitor even made many wagers on the outcome of our tournament games. Father was always sure of winning. But what does that have to do with everything that has transpired? What sequence of moves is he referring to? There are millions of possible moves in a game of chess. How are we supposed to answer that question? And if we were somehow able to answer it, what difference would it make? How would he even know that we had answered his question? From your reputation, I am sure you can see much deeper into the meaning of his second request. Please help us decipher the meaning of this request.

At this point, I do not know what to say. I know my father would be pleased if we can answer that question, but Reginald and I are so different, he has always been so business-minded, focusing on the end result, the bottom line, and pushing to expand the business. Our father was a shrewd businessman, and Reginald related to that part of him, but father also wanted to enjoy and experience life in any odd way that struck his fancy. He approached life on his own terms, no matter how strange or unconventional, if you understand what I mean. I was attracted to his free-spirited side and got along well with him in that regard.

Mr. Holmes, my brother and I are at a loss as to where to turn. If the missing funds are not found, I feel this will be the final rip in the relationship between my Reginald and myself. We have just lost our father, and to now lose the family fortune as well as each other, would be devastating. Can you help us in any way?

Sincerely,
Robert Rodricks

3rd letter
From the desk of
Robert Rodricks, MLS, LBR.

26 June, 1898

Dear Mr. Holmes,

My brother and I sincerely thank you for your response, and
for agreeing to investigate the missing funds. We have
spent considerable time discussing father's request in the
note that we discovered in the Queen of Hearts castle but
have yet to come up with a solution. We are still working
diligently on it, but chess is such a complex game, with so
many possibilities. It is a game of logic in the endgame, but
one of intuition and passion in the beginning of the game.
That is so very much describes father. He took so many
huge risks in building the family business to where he did,
And when I think of the outlandish bets he made with Mr.
Grabington on the tournament chess matches my bother and
I played, I can only say we were grateful that we did not
disappoint him. We just hope we can come through in his
final request.

Both of us were quite surprised that you wanted us to
reexamine father's yacht. And we were even more
surprised to discover that its halyard had been physically
tampered with. The broken ends of the wire rope did show
signs of a corrosive agent. The break was intentional, but
who would have done that? The vessel did sit in the boat
yard, unattended while it was hauled out for repairs, so
someone could have had access to it. We asked the boatyard
owner if he saw anyone near fathers' boat, and the only
thing he recalled was that father's old guide, Hans, did
come by several times looking for him saying something

about, he had a wonderful opportunity for a new sailing expedition. We contacted him and he offered his condolences and said that the few times he stopped by the boatyard, father was not there, so he simply waited by his boat for a while and then left. Returning to the halyard break, my observation, is that just rendering the mainsail unusable would not normally be that great a concern for an experienced sailor. Father could have very well returned to port using the jib and staysail alone. Being that his yacht is docked in slip number five, at the very end of the dock, he could have easily sailed right into the slip.

Based on the wire splicing tools, a crimper, snips, and wire sleeves, that were found on the cabin top, near the mast, he apparently did choose to attempt to repair it on the spot. Although it seems strange that the tools would still be there on the cabin top, when the boat had been rocking about in the waves for all that time. I cannot explain that, but that is where William said they were found. It is disheartening to know that if only he had waited to repair it until after he returned to the dock, he would still be with us now.

As per your request, I obtained and reviewed the invoices for the maintenance work that was recently done to "Checkmate" in the weeks prior to the accident. The material costs for the new blocks, name boards, steering wheel, and keel bolts were there, and proper. The labour for the installation of the purchased items, and a pre-painted, customer supplied new keel was also right for what was done. Apparently, the time that my father spent at his metal casting business, in the final week before it changed hands, was spent casting a new keel for his yacht. And rather than having the keel painted just prior to relaunching the yacht, as is typical, he had it painted with copper antifouling paint, before transporting it to the shipyard for installation. But then my father always had his own way of doing things.

In response to your question pertaining to his finances, the ones most familiar with his daily affairs were myself, my brother, Reginald, our butler, William, and regarding his financial affairs, his solicitor, Mr. Grabington, and Edward Granger, the clerk at the bank. When we discovered that father's funds were missing, I did visit the bank and spoke with Edward. I asked if he was aware of father possibly having moved his money to another account or even another institution. He replied, "I am typically not allowed to discuss a customer's financial concerns, but due to the nature of the situation, I can say that he did not move his funds to any other bank that I am aware of." I also inquired whether he knew of anyone else that would have knowledge regarding the amount of funds that father had been withdrawing. Again, he said, "I can not think of anyone outside our bank who would know". He said clearly that all the bank's customers' financial dealings are strictly private between the bank's customers and bank staff.

Perhaps Edward made a casual comment to someone about the large sums that father had been withdrawing. I imagine that would be rather unusual. I do know for a fact that Edward stops at the Bird in Hand pub every Friday for an end-of-the-work-week pint with his friends. From what I know, Edward's drinking associates include James Williamson, another bank clerk; his brother, Fredrick Granger, who works at the boat yard; and Benjamin Barns, the blacksmith and farrier who regularly tends to my family's carriage and horses.

Edward is a tall, well-built man in his late twenties, who has been a teller at the London County Bank for some years now, with an impeccable record. He seems like a decent chap. He was well aware of father's bank dealings. We cannot speak for the other teller, James, but his brother Fredrick was working with father on his boat repairs, so he would have had access to the vessel. He is the one who helped father and William in moving boxes from the shop to our home just before father sold the business and was quite pleased with the opportunity to earn some extra income. He too expressed his condolences but, they seemed rather halfhearted. Benjamin, our farrier, and blacksmith is quite the strapping fellow, and he has been working on our carriage a great deal as of late. The suspension has needed work several times recently, and besides that, our horses were in need of new shoes. He would have had free access to the exterior grounds of the house and the stable.

You also requested further information about the chess table and board located inside the Queen of Hearts castle in the Wonderland Garden. I looked through the invoices for the garden project and discovered that the table and chess board were made by Waring & Gillow, a cabinet and furniture design and manufacturing company that does a variety of metal and woodwork, including fine inlays, locking mechanism, and intricate clockworks. The purchase was listed as a 'custom one-off, hand-made table with chess board, including magnetised chess pieces and special, inlaid features.' I believe that the 'specific features' refers to the intricate inlaid design upon its surface. Prior to his disappearance, father and I had played several games on the new Queen of Hearts table and board. I did notice that while we played, father seemed to be listening intently and seemed quite pleased with the new board. And he was smiling happily during all of those games.

Your final question inquired about William's usual itinerary. Since father's accident, he still tends to the house, although there is not as much to do. He no longer has to provide transportation for our father, so instead he goes down to the harbour every day to clean and verify the status of 'Checkmate' and the family's motor yacht, 'Herald of the Morning.' The two are docked right next to each other. He has taken to bringing some lunch with him and spending the afternoon just staring at 'Checkmate', as if he could bring father back somehow. He also brings the daily news paper to the harbour with him, and oddly enough, one day, I did observe him bringing one of father's wool sailing sweaters. I asked him about that, and he nervously replied that it was for sentimental reasons, that he felt it belonged on the boat. He felt so bad about the broken halyard that at least he could keep a part of father on boat. I did not know how to respond, so I said to go ahead and take it.

One final note is that father's solicitor, Mr. Grabington has inquired several times, if we wish to sell father's sailing yacht. He said he truly understands that it would be a constant reminder of father's disappearance, and how we had really failed him so badly, as sons in getting along. It would be so much easier for us if we just sold it to him, and we should just sell the boat and move on. He said, he could give us a particularly good price for it, which would be a considerable help to us, since the missing funds have not been found. We are considering his offer, but are not yet ready to make that move, as we first want to honour father's final request with the last game of chess. Perhaps that will answer our questions.

I do believe that addresses all your requests for information. My brother and I, for the first time in ages, are managing to work together somewhat peaceably, and have together searched both the house and the Wonderland Garden one final time, but with no success. We have come to agreement that the funds are not hidden in either of those locations, and neither one of us are responsible. Your various queries are intriguing, and we do hope that they may provide insights into who really made off with his funds. We pray that you find an answer to this before the money has been altogether lost.

Attached is the invoice from the Ships Chandlery for the equipment and labour, on father's yacht. Also attached is a letter from a naval architect, which we found attached to the Chandlery invoice.

Sincerely,
Robert Rodericks
Reginald Rodericks

Westmore and Co. Ltd.
Ship's Chandlery
20 Swain Street,
London,

Invoice 413   2 June, 1898
Reginald Rodricks Junior
Yacht "Checkmate"

2 #7 jib sheet blocks @ 2.25 each   4.50
1 set #7 main sheet blocks @ 6.70
1 set #5 mizzen sheet blocks @ 4.70
4 sets brass chocks and cleats @ 8.00   32.00
1 nickel plated mahogany steering wheel @ 15.00
2 mahogany name boards with brass letters @ 2.50   5.00
1 set new keel bolts @ 13.00
Total parts 53.20

Labour for installation of purchased items 10 shillings
Labour for installation of customer supplied new keel 3
shillings
Labour for redesign calculations of new keel 25.00
shillings
Total 78.20 + 13 shillings

PAID IN FULL

From the desk of Chadwick Halsey Herringbone, Naval Architect

Dear Mr. Rodericks,

I have completed the calculations for designing and casting a new keel for your sailing yacht, the 'Checkmate' per your request, changing the mass density of the keel material from 11.4g/cc to 19.3 g/cc, and keeping the keel bolt pattern exactly the same. They have had them delivered to you at your foundry. This should improve the performance of your vessel, although it is rather unconventional.

Sincerely,
Chadwick Halsey Herringbone, Naval Architect

4th Letter

From the desk of
Robert Rodricks, MLS, LBR.
28 June, 1898

Dear Mr. Holmes,

We received your reply to our last letter, and followed your suggestion, that we look further into Edward, the bank teller, his friend Benjamin Barns, and father's solicitor, Mr. Grabington. First, we talked with the bank manager, a Mr. Donald McPhearson. He said that all of father's cash withdrawals which Edward processed, were reviewed and approved by the manager, and Edward followed standard bank procedure on each of the transactions. He also said that Edward's work record and performance have been exemplary, although he did note that Edward does regularly stop at the pub every Friday after work and spends a considerable amount of time there.

Looking into Benjamin was a similar story. We talked with several of his other customers, and they all agreed that he has done an outstanding job for them, always being punctual, doing excellent work, charging fair prices, and never skimping on quality. He is known to be very congenial, and good natured, and his long-time familiarity with our family do speak highly for him as well. Ben has been a reliable blacksmith and farrier for us over the years, and I know father trusted him, but it does seem strange that he has had to repair the carriage suspension as often as he has recently done. He has spent a great deal of time here at the house in the weeks before father's disappearance, and to my knowledge, has had a significant amount of freedom going about the grounds.

Regarding Mr. Grabington, we made some discrete inquiries and learned that in addition to making many bets with our father over the years, as we have previously mentioned, he apparently has quite a habit of betting on various things with his other clients, which he seemed to have kept very well hidden, until we investigated. We were only able to learn of this by talking directly to his other clients and appealing to their sympathies regarding our father's passing. It appears that in-spite of his successful solicitor business, he owes betting debt money to several other of his clients. Yet, he has still very insistent in asking us to sell the 'Checkmate' to him, that we should act quickly, or we will soon be out of funds if we do not.

Regarding your question regarding William's eating habits, I have never paid them much attention, but I did observe him preparing his lunch today. His appetite seems to be quite hearty, as he prepared himself several sandwiches of cold beef and cotswold cheese on rye bread. He also packed several small cakes and fresh fruit. I confess that the meal reminded me of afternoons with my father. Reginald and I looked forward to meals with him because he always insisted on fresh fruit, regardless of the occasion.

Finally, in consideration of my father's request in the last message that we received from him, Reginald and I have done as he asked, and played a game of chess upon the Queen of Hearts' chess board. We realised that based on his question, "With Knight to QB3, as the opening move, what is the optimum number of following moves that would please me?", it would seem that he wanted us to stop our rivalry and competition and just play to a draw. Reginald and I had never played to a draw. Neither one of us would have previously ever considered such an idea. It was always win or lose. However, over the last several days of working together, trying to find an answer, we seem to have come to some kind of truce, and we felt that playing the chess game to a draw, would honour father's last wish. Not to mention, we both hoped to find some sort of answer regarding his request, and maybe another clue as to what happened to the funds. So, we started a game, with the opening move as stated in the message. I did open with Knight, to Queen's Bishop 3. Since father's request stated, emphatically, that we should play the game in the optimum, or least possible number of moves, that would mean of course, it would be a simple threefold occurrence of position, the chess rule, where when all of the pieces are in the exact same position three times in the game, a draw can be requested and accepted, thus ending the game. The shortest number of moves in which that can be accomplished, with a Queen's Knight opening, totals five moves. It would be two moves each out, two moves each back, and the fifth move out, completing the threefold occurrence. Then one of us requests the draw, and the other accepts it, ending the game. In truth it is simple, but then no one wants to play to draw. There is no purpose in that, unless, of course, you are playing in a tournament, are comfortably ahead, and can afford the draws. But then, that certainly does not apply to our father's request.

Reginald then opened with his knight to King's Bishop 3. In the second move, we then returned our knights to their previous positions. In the third move, we repeated the opening move, and in the fourth move, we again returned our knights to their original positions. Mr. Holmes, you have no idea the restraint it took to make that last series of moves. We had never played to a draw in our entire lives.

We stared in silence at each other, with me wondering if I should continue playing to a draw, and wondering if Reginald would do the same, or should just play forward and attack. Then, as I started the fifth move, again moving my Knight to Queen's Bishop 3, I was almost certain that I heard a faint mechanical clicking inside the chess table. And when Reginald moved his knight to King's Bishop 3, completing the threefold occurrence of position, there was more clicking, like the sound of mechanical gears moving. The anticipation and suspense we felt at that moment was immeasurable. And then, one of the inlaid decorative panels of the table opened to reveal the number "five." That was it! Nothing more. I will be honest, we both thought that when we heard the sound of gears moving, it would open some secret panel revealing the hidden funds, or at least directions to where they are located, but no, just a simple number "five." There was no note, or letter of explanation, or anything. Just the number "five." After the initial shock and disappointment, we actually broke into laughter for a moment. We were dumbfounded! All that for just a number!

I was at a total loss, and Reginald was just staring at the number, when suddenly, it came to him. That is when he pointed out that father's sailing yacht, "Checkmate," is docked in slip number five at the harbour. We thought, perhaps that there must be an additional clue that we had missed, still hidden somewhere on board the yacht, that would lead us to his fortune. I will say that we rushed down to the harbour and spent the rest of the day searching in earnest, but to no avail. We searched the yacht from bow to stern and looked in every locker and hatch. We checked the ship's logbook and all the navigation books on board but found nothing. We even were sure to look particularly close at page five of every book or periodical on board. We scraped the polished finish on the cowlings and some of the other fittings, but there was nothing under the surface. We did not find anything. The only thing we noticed while sitting in the cockpit after our futile search efforts, is that the cabin drapes on my father's motor yacht, 'Herald of the Morning' were closed. William probably left them that way after his lunch. He has seemed rather distracted lately.

As disappointed as we were, I will say, that even though we did not find any clues to the missing funds, there was a certain satisfaction in neither winning nor losing, and just finally working together. In fact, we actually shook hands for the first time in decades. We really do think father would have been quite pleased. But the fact still stands that his fortune has vanished, and that there is something missing that we have yet to see in all this. We both implore you, as we are at our wit's end, and have nowhere to turn. and we are in full agreement on this. Please help us!

Sincerely,
Robert Rodricks
Reginald Rodricks

5th Letter

221-b Baker Street
London, England
Sherlock Holmes
Consulting Detective

30 June, 1898

Dear Robert and Reginald,

I am quite pleased to have aided the both of you in working together to resolve the disappearance of your father's fortune, as well as receiving the cryptic reward mentioned in his will, one that was even greater than either of you could have imagined.

In this particular case, although it was straightforward for me to determine one aspect of exactly what was going on, there was another side, that was hidden deeper and required additional consideration. This case has provided a great deal of satisfaction, in knowing that you two are finally working together, and have become a true family. Being that I left as soon as everything was resolved, I am writing this letter to explain a few of the finer points of this adventure.

As far as solving the question of the missing funds, based on the first letter, from Reginald, I was almost certain that they had not been absconded with, but merely hidden by your father. It was obvious that he wanted you both to finally get over your rivalry and work together, as indicated by the numerous previous attempts to get you two to work together that he had mentioned. But there was much more to this situation than was obvious. His rivalry and betting with his solicitor had grown over the years, and even though he was disappointed in one aspect of you two, he was also fiercely certain of your ability to eventually work together, solve the riddle, play the game of chess and therefore, determine where the funds were located. It was a huge gamble, his greatest ever in a lengthy line of risky unorthodox decisions that he had made over the course of his life, but one he was certain he would win. Mr. Grabington was secretly getting deeper in debt from his betting problem and wanted to come up with a scheme to take advantage of your father's risk-taking nature, and his total confidence in the both of you. That is why he was repeatedly asking you to sell the boat to him. Solicitors, by nature can be very convincing and manipulative, and he convinced your father to take a bet on his entire fortune, that you would both succeed, in working together even though it seemed that all of his fortune had somehow disappeared. Your father's shouting, "You can bet on it!" was a clear sign of his confidence, and you did not fail him. Of course, based on everything you shared, your father was a huge risk taker no matter how extreme or unreasonable it may have been.

He created this entire scheme to prove his love and confidence in you both, as well as to prove a point to Mr. Grabington. The statement in the will that specifically referred to his disappearance was a clue that there was something else going on. That the will would be invoked even in the case of his disappearance, indicated to me that he had orchestrated the disappearance of the funds. The first question was where were the funds hidden? From the initial description in Reginald's letter, it pointed to the painted Wonderland Garden statues, and the Queen of Hearts castle building, especially since it was located in the centre of the garden, but that was quickly disproved. However, his wordplay in his second message, regarding getting to the "bottom" of the matter, was another clue that there was more to the mystery than initially appeared.

The letters from Robert, expounded on that, going into much greater detail pertaining to the actual disappearance of your father, and the fact that considerable work had been done to his sailing yacht, especially the new keel. It would make sense that if one wanted to hide a large amount of gold, and one had a metal-casting facility at his disposal, then what better way to hide it, than to cast a new keel of gold. The weight of your father's fortune in gold, which is heavier than lead, the typical material used for sailboat ballast keels, is sufficient so it would work perfectly, but it it would require a redesign of the keel and is much more obvious in its surface appearance. That is why, the fact that the keel had been pre-painted with copper bottom paint before being transported to the boatyard for installation, and the letter from the naval architect confirmed my suspicion.

Your suspicions regarding Benjamin being involved were reasonable, but in truth, your father's carriage did need work on the suspension. This was due to the fact that he had been transporting the gold to his metal casting business to make the new keel.

Dr. Hardegan is still seeking investors for his time machine project, and from what I understand, really believes he can make it happen. However, based on logic and fact, I do not see that ever happening.

Hans was just seeking added business opportunities from a proven source, and from what I have learned has succeeded.

The fact that William helped your father cast the new keel and was the only one to discover your father's disappearance, did indicate that he was an integral part of your father's plan. The tools and wire splicing sleeves on the cabin top were planted by William, and you were right to question how they could be there considering the motion of the vessel. However, if Reginald Junior had planned to disappear, and pretend to be missing while you two were solving his riddles. Where could he safely hide? It had to seem that he had fallen overboard from the sailing yacht. So, when William met him, far out of sight from anyone on land, your father simply hid in one of the interior cabins of his motor yacht, while William towed the "Checkmate" back to port. That provided the illusion of his drowning and gave him a hiding place while you two solved the questions he presented. While all the attention was focused on his sailing yacht, 'Checkmate', the family house, and the Wonderland Garden, he was comfortably staying in the cabin of his motor yacht. William had taken to having his lunch aboard the yacht, providing your father with his daily meals, and a status of how you were both doing. Of course, his edginess and bringing one of your father's sweaters to the boat, was further indication of what was going on. The motor yacht has all the conveniences of a small house, with total privacy, and a view of the proceedings with the sailing yacht which was moored in slip number "5." And of course, the number "five," was the answer to his riddle in the second message, given the stated opening, Knight to QB3, what are the least number of chess moves that would please him.

The answer was obviously for you both to play to a draw, invoking the threefold occurrence of pieces rule, in five moves. It would show that you had gotten over your rivalry and were finally cooperating. Especially since you

142

mentioned that the two of you had never in your lives played a game of chess against each other to a draw. But the question now, was how to lead you to the answer once you did achieve that level of cooperation. The answer was to have the chess board fabricated, such that the movement of the magnetised pieces functioned like a locking mechanism and when completed, opened the panel revealing the number five, the slip number of his yacht. The Wonderland Garden was an elaborate setting of the stage, with the Queen of Hearts castle, special table and chess board being the key factors.

When I met the two of you aboard his yacht, after I received your last letter, I reminded you that per his message, your father wanted you to get to the "bottom" of the matter. I must say that it was most satisfying to see the two of you look at each other, finally make the realisation, and both exclaim at the same time, "The keel!" When you both tore off your shirts, trousers and shoes, and dove into the water to scrape off a bit of bottom paint to verify that was the case, I enjoyed watching your father, who was happily observing from the cabin of the motor yacht. His satisfaction was even more obvious when you resurfaced and saw him standing there on the dock. The two of you had succeeded in solving his riddles, and in doing so, received a reward even greater than either of you could have imagined. Your father has returned to you. His elaborate ruse and considerable risk had succeeded in finally bringing the two of you together and locating the family fortune. He was well aware that if you and both given up and sold the Checkmate to Mr. Grabington the fortune would have been lost, but that was a risk he was willing to take, the end of an extensive line of risks. It turns out, that having lost his final bet with your father, his debts have caught up with him and he is facing the consequences.

I understand that with the gold now accounted for, the business sold, and your father safely returned, you have decided to all go on an extended family cruise together, from what I understand with Hans, from the 'Hans will get you there. Guide Service' as your navigator. I wish you smooth sailing, and successful teamwork.

Sincerely,
Sherlock Holmes

However Improbable

Watson sat in contemplation,
wondering what to do.
Sherlock sighed in affirmation,
saying that it's true.

"When you have eliminated,
through precise deduction,
the impossible, you'll be elated.
There will be no obstruction.

For then whatever does remain,
however improbable,
or strange, or odd, or even arcane,
it's not just probable.

It must be 'truth', I say.
I know that it is so.
Mark my words this very day,
as onward you do go.

Use these words as your guide
in all you come across.
The answer then will never hide.
You'll ne'er be at a loss."

Watson nodded, "Yes, I see.
Your words they are quite true.
A bit verbose, if you ask me.
To recall, hard to do.

When you have eliminated
excess words and rhyme,
then it will be abbreviated
to a shorter line.

Keep it simple and precise,
easy to remember.
Short and sweet and quite concise
like a burning ember."

"Watson, you are brilliant!"
Sherlock then replied.
"Your words they are resilient,
and can not be denied."

A one-line phrase for all time,
a true deduction tool!
It will solve most any crime.
A simple basic rule.

Here it is my trusted friend.
Tell me what you think.
This will be the perfect end.
We'll put it down in ink."

"When you have eliminated all which is impossible, then
whatever remains, however improbable, must be the
truth."